TAKE IT

In all too many man-woman relationships, it is the woman who longs for marriage and a family and the man who doesn't want to be committed to anything long-term. In the case of Zee Robertson and Lorn Jensen, however, it was the other way around: he wanted to settle down and she was only interested in her career. Which one would give way?

Books you will enjoy
by ELIZABETH OLDFIELD

FLORIDA FEVER

Nicole might have been wealthy once, but she certainly wasn't now, which was why she had been relieved to get the job working for Drew Benedict in Florida. But nothing would convince Drew that she wasn't a 'rich bitch'. Nevertheless, in view of his almost lethal attraction, wouldn't it be safer to let him go on thinking that way?

SECOND TIME AROUND

Returning to Singapore for the first time since her beloved husband Patrick had died was a rather sad experience for Leigh—but there were old friends to welcome her and make her stay a happy one. But there was also Jake St John, who had been responsible for Patrick's death . . .

DREAM HERO

Two years ago, T.V. personality Bryce Cameron had cruelly played on reporter Caitlin Saunders' inexperience, and now she was all set for revenge. Her resolve started to crumble, though, when she was faced with Bruce's considerable charm. But she had no intention of becoming just another in a long line of girls . . .

SUBMISSION

Most girls would have given their eye teeth to marry the pop star Shane Santiago—but not Rhiannon. All her love had been given to her fiancé Brad and she was still grieving over his death. Yet if the pop group on which they all depended were not to disintegrate, marry Shane she must!

TAKE IT
OR LEAVE IT

BY
ELIZABETH OLDFIELD

MILLS & BOON LIMITED
15–16 BROOK'S MEWS
LONDON W1A 1DR

First published 1983
Australian copyright 1983
Philippine copyright 1984
This edition 1984

© Elizabeth Oldfield 1983

ISBN 0 263 74476 0

Set in Monophoto Times 10 on 10½ pt.
01-0184 – 59337

Made and printed in Great Britain by
Richard Clay (The Chaucer Press) Ltd,
Bungay, Suffolk

CHAPTER ONE

ZEE stabbed a slender finger at the typewriter. Damn! Now she had gone and hit the wrong key. Looping a strand of flaming red hair behind her ear, she reached for the correction fluid. Typing wasn't her forte, she thought, scowling at the pile of blank menu cards. What crazy impulse had prompted her to prepare fresh ones, when fresh ones weren't really needed? She sighed. There was nothing deadlier than striving to give the appearance of being busily involved when, in truth, there wasn't a single worthwhile thing to do. If only it was in her nature to abandon the pretence and be honestly idle. Cat-green eyes wandered to Heather, sprawled in a chair by the reception desk knitting happily, humming beneath her breath. But Heather had an excuse. In her bulging maternity dress she was the picture of contented sloth.

Zee blew on the white splodge. Initially life at the Greenan Towers Hotel had seemed a welcome relief from her usual frenzied pace, but it had palled in double-quick time. Casting a shrewd glance around the shabby wood-panelled hall, she assessed it to be a home for retired misfits, for almost without exception the staff mooched around with a somnolent air. They were totally devoid of any urge to quicken their pace. Not that their pace needed to quicken, she thought cynically. Indeed, once the few guests had stumbled in through the revolving doors, they too drifted into a mood of listlessness. Her finger prodded again, successfully this time. She was a misfit herself, out of place with her craving for excitement and activity.

'By the way,' Heather remarked, reaching the end of a row, 'there was a reservation in the post for a single. I suppose it ought to be prepared.'

'I'll go upstairs and tell Molly,' Zee offered with a smile, delighted at the chance of a diversion.

'Thanks.' Although she had made no attempt to rise, Heather shuffled herself even deeper into her chair. 'If I grow any bigger I'll not be able to squeeze through the door,' she said, patting her tummy, 'let alone climb the stairs.'

'Only six more weeks.'

'Thank goodness! It must have been a man who said pregnancy was fun—swollen ankles and an extra twenty pounds to carry around. They'll be bringing me here in a wheelbarrow if I last the course.'

'You will.' Zee was encouraging.

'I hope so. I do need the money. Mr McCrimmon was very kind, allowing me to stay on. He's a wee sweetie.'

Too sweet and too soft-hearted, Zee categorised, but remained silent.

'What I'd give to have a day, just a single day, slender again like you,' Heather sighed, uncomfortably shifting her weight. 'I love your outfit. Did you buy it in London?'

Zee nodded. City-slicker smart, the pale caramel silk suit fitted to perfection, pencil-slim skirt clinging to her hips. Beneath the long-sleeved jacket she wore a tailored cream blouse. The colours had been painstakingly chosen to complement the exotic blaze of her hair. Good grooming was important to Zee. Her clothes were expensive, always immaculate and, she had to admit, far too chic for her present surroundings.

'I'll ask Molly and Agnes to clean Room Eight, shall I?' she queried, making for the wide wooden staircase.

'Yes, please.'

She paused when she reached the landing. The corridor stretched to the left and halfway down stood a tall figure, motionless beside the bay window. Him again! she thought irritably. He was a misfit too. There was no hint of aimlessness about *his* approach. Although he had arrived only the previous morning the man had already made his presence felt—and how! Spending most of his time on the prowl in the corridors and public rooms, or walking around the outside of the building, he had never left the grounds, and his constant presence was in the process of unsettling everyone. Twice she had disturbed him in the lounge. He had been jotting down notes, deep in concentration. On her approach he had snapped his book closed and glared at her so coldly she had felt impelled to retreat as though she was an intruder. Zee squared her shoulders. How could you hope to deal equably with such a disgruntled guest? His expression indicated, beyond all doubt, that his opinion of Greenan Towers was low. Very low. Why does he stay here? she wondered. Why doesn't he move on? Nothing pleased him. He had complained that the central heating was difficult to regulate, that the bar service was slow, that the porterage facility was non-existent. Old Jimmy, the porter, *had* been summoned, but never materialised, and after waiting in vain for several minutes the man had carried his own suitcase— with bad grace. Zee suspected Jimmy had been warming his bones against the boiler, as usual, ignoring all shouts.

The man rested a foot on the window seat, knee bent, and thrust a hand in his trouser pocket, jacket falling free. Not moving a muscle, and he had plenty, he examined the view. He probably didn't approve of that, either! In his pale grey suit, with wide shoulders and ramrod straight back, he reminded her of a granite statue. His heart was doubtless stone, too. They should stick him on a plinth beside Robbie Burns in the square, Zee thought peevishly, then he won't be able to bother us any more. But whereas Robbie Burns, Scotland's favourite poet, had had dark hair and a pleasant expression, this man was stern-faced and blond. Very blond.

'Perhaps he bleaches it, plenty of men do these days,' Aileen, the young waitress, had giggled nervously. Already she had felt the lash of his tongue and had sought out Zee and Heather for a spot of comfort.

'Don't be a wee daftie,' Heather had said. 'Can you imagine a macho man like him sitting under the drier with his hair in tinfoil?'

The three of them had chuckled at the ridiculous image. He was aggressively masculine, conservative in his dress and certainly not a man to be concerned about a triviality such as the colour of his hair.

'He's a hunk—a gorgeous hunk,' Heather had continued, but she added, 'in a severe kind of way.'

Much too severe, Zee reasoned. His face would crack if he smiled. Let's hope he moves on soon, she thought, wondering what errors he would discover this morning. Perversely most of her annoyance stemmed from the uneasy acknowledgement that his complaints were justified. Greenan Towers was sloppily run, but even so she resented the distinct satisfaction he took in pinpointing one fault after another. Forcing herself to ignore a flutter of apprehension at having to approach, she walked forward. Pop music was blaring from an open door beyond him, where Molly and Agnes, the two chambermaids, were making up the beds.

'Good morning, sir,' she said brightly, drawing level.

He remained immobile, eyes fixed unblinkingly on the wind-buffeted trees in the garden. He's going to ignore me, she realised when there was no reply. Anger blazed through her. What an objectionable character he was! But as she passed by he spoke, suddenly.

'What's the total acreage of the grounds?'

Surprised, she came to a halt, swinging round. 'I'm afraid I really have no idea, sir.'

His profile was forbidding, arrow-straight nose and clean-cut jaw. A thick moustache, as fair as his hair, covered his top lip. He was taller than most men. Zee topped six foot in her high heels, but even she was forced to look up to him.

He turned to confront her. 'No idea?' He sounded incredulous that such a fact wasn't at her fingertips. Zee bridled. He barked out a second question. 'Does the strip of land between the rear fence and the wall belong to the hotel?'

Her eyes travelled across the wide sweep of the lawns to the distant tumbledown wooden fence and the stone wall a few yards beyond. Behind the wall were windswept sand-dunes and grey sea stretching to the horizon.

'Yes, sir.' She was tempted to add, 'Though it's none of your business,' but stopped herself. Her training was too strong. Staff were not allowed to answer back, however great the provocation.

'And what is it used for?'

'A vegetable garden, sir.'

Thick blond brows were raised. 'Vegetables!' There was a disbelieving grunt. 'But the ground is derelict.'

'It *is* November,' she emphasised frostily. 'There's not much growing just now.'

'And by springtime you'd have me believe the plot groans with lush crops?' His mouth curved into a sneer.

'I really have no idea, sir,' she replied, starting to turn away, needing to escape from the sarcasm which riled.

'No idea?' There was a crusty layer of scorn. 'Can you tell me if there's a resident gardener?' He sounded as though he didn't expect her to know about that, either, but this time she was sure of her facts.

'Yes, sir,' she said, a rebellious gleam in the depths of her emerald eyes. 'Old Jimmy, the porter, tends the garden.'

'The invisible man,' he crowed. 'Well, he seems to be as efficient at horticulture as he is at porterage. The garden is a disaster!'

Zee was stung into retaliation. 'He *is* almost seventy.'

'Then why the hell isn't he retired?' the man snapped.

She glared at him, lost for an explanation.

'I really have no idea, sir,' he mimicked cruelly, making her flush. 'You don't seem to have ideas about most things, Miss—er——?'

'Miss Robertson,' she supplied through gritted teeth. 'The reason I'm not a walking encyclopedia is that I've only worked here for three months.' She paused and added a sardonic 'sir'. Her hair wasn't red for nothing. This inquisitive stranger was creeping under her skin and she didn't like it. Not one bit.

'Where did you work before?'

'In London,' she said briefly.

'Where in London?'

Zee took a steadying breath. He was too damn nosey! 'At the Ecrepoint Hotel, and if you would excuse me, sir, I have work to do.' She was poised to leave.

'The Ecrepoint,' he arched a brow, obviously impressed. 'Quite a change for you, coming here?'

'Yes, sir.'

There was a burst of shared laughter from the open bedroom door farther along the corridor.

'Chambermaids wouldn't get away with such unruly behaviour at the Ecrepoint,' he grimaced, taking a slim gold cigarettte case from his inside jacket pocket. 'Too noisy and too long-winded.'

'Yes, sir.'

He flipped open the case and offered it to her. 'Smoke?'

'No, thank you.'

'Not while you're on duty?' he asked, placing a cigarette between his lips.

'Never.'

Lighting the cigarette from the flame of a gold lighter, he inhaled. 'Those two should be split up,' he pronounced, jerking his fair head in the direction of the bedroom where Molly and Agnes were giggling. 'They would work far quicker alone.'

'That's true.'

He pulled down the corners of his mouth in a gesture of surprise at her agreement, and took another drag at his cigarette. 'And that damn radio should be forbidden. Someone could be trying to rest in the next room. The noise they're making would waken the dead!'

'Yes, sir,' she nodded.

'Well, if you agree with what I'm saying why don't you do something about it?' he barked, propelling her into a backwards step at the unexpected force of his attack.

'Me?' she asked in surprise.

After a momentary lull, the hard glint of battle had returned to his blue eyes. They were ice-cold. Zee suppressed a shudder.

'The rest of the staff don't have the first idea about serving the public,' he retorted staring out at the garden again, his profile taut with annoyance.

'But it's not my place to interfere,' she said.

'Why not?' He rounded on her. 'What the hell are you, anyway? What do you do, apart from running errands on behalf of that pregnant lady downstairs?'

She tightened her lips. 'I act as relief receptionist and do some secretarial work for Mr McCrimmon, the manager.'

'Are you and the other girl on split shifts?'

'Well—er—no, sir,' she waffled. He was about to make another justified complaint, she thought wearily. She was on the losing side, and she knew it. 'The hotel is usually quiet in the evenings. Mr McCrimmon keeps an eye out for the reception counter then.'

He gave a bark of derision. ''Struth! There are only half a dozen guests. Why are two receptionists required, especially both working at the same time?'

Zee had had enough. 'I really have no idea, sir,' she said crisply, taking malicious satisfaction in her defiance. 'I suggest you ask Mr McCrimmon himself.'

Pivoting, she marched away. He watched her go, enjoying the sway of her hips as she disappeared to speak with the chambermaids. That one knows what it's all about, he decided, she'll be useful. He allowed himself a moment's relaxation. Red hair and green eyes, he reflected. I'll bet she's a wildcat when she's roused!

He had disappeared when Zee returned to the corridor. It was a relief. She ran down the stairs and crossed the parquet floor towards the reception desk, high heels smartly rapping. Aileen was chatting with Heather and turned at the sound.

Zee came to an abrupt halt. 'What have you done with your hair?' she asked in a horrified voice.

Aileen's nondescript looks were now highlighted with flecks of neon pink. 'Do you like it?' The girl slid a hand to the back of her neck, lifting the long strands.

'It's different,' Zee admitted as she approached to have a closer look.

'Gary wanted me to be in fashion,' Aileen announced smugly.

Zee knew that if Gary, Aileen's boy-friend, had told her to shave her head she would have complied without a murmur.

'And that's fashion?' Heather queried from her perch, eyes sparkling with amusement.

Doubtfully Aileen squinted at her reflection in the glass of a photograph hung on the wall. 'Perhaps it is a bit bright.'

'Has Mr McCrimmon seen you yet?' Zee enquired. 'What was his reaction?'

'He didn't like it. He said the colour wasn't suitable, me working in a public place and all.' Aileen tossed back her head, pink hair dancing. 'Och, he's an old fuddy-duddy!'

Zee was impelled to have her say, even though she was risking unpopularity. 'I agree with him. You'd never be allowed to work in any other hotel with hair that colour.'

'Whatever will Lorn Jensen think?' Heather asked with a mischievous chuckle.

'Lorn Jensen?' Zee was unable to tear her eyes away from the horrendous hair.

'Our ultra-friendly guest.'

She nodded, remembering his name now. 'He'll go bananas,' she prophesied.

'What I do with my hair is my own business, it's nothing to do with him,' Aileen said belligerently, then her face fell. 'Is it?'

'No, of course not. Don't worry.' Zee oozed confidence. 'I've just had a confrontation with him myself, and emerged intact.' She lifted the hinged counter top and walked through to her desk. 'He really disapproves of the hotel. I wonder why he stays here?'

'I can't understand it either,' Heather agreed, shaking her head. 'He arrived out of the blue yesterday morning, without a reservation. How did he know Greenan Towers existed? We're tucked away off the main road, out of the centre of Ayr. He'd never find us if he was merely passing through.'

'Perhaps he saw an advertisement,' Aileen suggested, slumping against the counter into her favourite position. She had been known to spend hours propped up there, gossiping.

Zee pulled a face. 'I doubt it. Mr McCrimmon doesn't advertise much, especially at this time of year.'

'Maybe he's here for the horse-racing,' Heather contributed.

Aileen scowled. 'I hope not. It's ten days before the next meeting. Heaven help us if we have to suffer him all that time.'

'It's not the races.' Thoughtfully Zee revolved a pencil between her fingers. 'I'm sure he has an ulterior motive. He hasn't been off the premises since he arrived, and he's extremely curious about how the hotel operates. I was given the seventh degree just now.'

'Perhaps he's from one of the motoring organisations, doing an annual check,' Heather commented. 'Or from a good food guide.'

Zee shook her head. 'He's too classy for that. I doubt their men would drive a pale bronze Porsche.'

Cross-eyed, Aileen was examining a strand of neon hair. 'Gary says the car must have cost a bomb, but *he'd* rather have a motorbike.'

'Gary would.' Heather's retort was flat.

Zee tapped the end of the pencil on her sharp white teeth. 'I have a feeling I've seen him before, but I can't think where.'

Heather ran her finger down the register. 'It says "Lorn Jensen, London." Jensen sounds Scandinavian. Perhaps that accounts for his fair hair.'

'He doesn't sound foreign to me,' Aileen grumbled. 'He just sounds cross.'

Zee and Heather laughed. A door at the rear of the hall opened and Mr McCrimmon, a thickset man in his late fifties, poked out his head. 'Zee, could you bring your notebook? I have some letters to be typed,' he shouted.

She gathered up pad and pencil. 'Why don't you check that the tables are laid for lunch?' she suggested as she passed Aileen. The girl grimaced at the task, but moved reluctantly away towards the dining-room.

When Zee entered his office Mr McCrimmon was standing at a grey metal cabinet, rifling through the files. He sighed, raising his hands in despair. 'The Chairman, Edgar Devenay, has been on the telephone,' he told her. 'He wants a complete breakdown of our running costs for the past year—wants it quickly. It'll be a time-consuming task. I hardly know where to start.'

'I'll help,' Zee offered impetuously, not having a clue what was involved. 'Give me a list of the different headings he requires and I'll sort out the figures.'

'It's not as easy as that,' the manager confessed. 'The files are incomplete, half the knowledge is up here.' He tapped the side of his head. 'I always manage to sort things out with the accountants because George is a friend of mine. He moves in for a week each year, and we muddle through. An itemised breakdown for submission to headquarters is entirely another matter.' He sat down heavily, facing her across the desk. 'Normally we don't have much contact with the London office. Mr Edgar allows me to run things my own way.' He lowered his voice. 'Between you and me, Greenan Towers barely breaks even. The other hotels in the Devenay empire must be carrying it.'

'Altogether there are twenty-five in the chain, aren't there?' she asked.

He nodded. 'Half a dozen in London, ten others spread throughout the U.K., some in the States, and one or two in the Far East and the Caribbean.'

'Why has this place never been modernised?' Zee glanced around the untidy office. Like the rest of the hotel it was in dire need of attention. In its day the heavy old furniture would have been splendid, but now, along with the worn carpets and antique plumbing, it left much to be desired. 'If I was given a free hand I'd gut the whole building and start again from scratch.'

'So would I,' Mr McCrimmon agreed, settling back in his chair. Zee could tell he was about to embark on his daily preamble. Whenever he called her into his office he devoted the majority of his time to conversation, fitting dictation into the last five minutes.

'Greenan Towers has been kept like this for sentimental reasons,' he explained. 'Mr Robert, Edgar's father always had a soft spot in his heart for it. He never wanted things to change. Edgar has carried on the tradition. Mr Robert used to tell me how Greenan Towers was one of the first hotels his father, Angus Devenay, opened. Apparently Mr Robert spent many happy childhood holidays here.' He smiled nostalgically. 'What a great character that man was! He had a rich booming voice and, my word, when he said "jump", everyone jumped. He was very shrewd, too.' He shook his head. 'Edgar's not at all like him, must take after his mother.'

'Is Mr Robert still alive?' she asked, drawn into the tale.

'Och no, lassie. He died about twelve years ago, I'm sorry to say.' He tapped stubby fingers against his chin. 'Let's see now, Edgar must be around forty-five and his two sisters, Margaret and Helen, will be approaching forty.'

'Are the sisters involved in the running of the Devenay chain?'

'Good heavens, no!' He sounded so shocked at the idea of women playing such a role that Zee smiled.

'I imagine they own shares,' he said, 'but it's Mr Edgar who runs the show. Mind you, business hasn't been prospering. He's not a strong Chairman, like his father. I mean,' he waved a hand vaguely, 'fancy allowing a set-up like this to soldier on!'

She suppressed a comment, marvelling that the manager could carelessly disclaim any responsibility for the state of the hotel when he had worked there all his life, many years of which in the capacity of supremo. Steepling his fingers, Mr McCrimmon continued. 'From what Mr Edgar said on the phone, it sounds as though changes could be imminent. He suggested I try and smarten things up. He's intending to pay us a visit before Christmas.'

'Perhaps he'll close Greenan Towers,' Zee suggested. It would be a sensible decision. She doubted that the finances were anywhere near breaking even as the manager had said. A loss seemed more probable. The register had shown a dearth of reservations all summer. Often there had been more staff than guests.

'Good heavens, I hope not!' Mr McCrimmon paled, grasping the edge of the desk. 'There are only six more years until I retire, and I'd never find another job at my age. Greenan Towers is all I know.' He wrinkled his brow. 'What would you do to improve matters? You've been trained in hotel management. You've worked in a five-star London hotel. What changes would you make?'

Zee crossed her legs, adjusting her skirt at her knees as she considered his question.

'Leaving aside the obvious ones of spending vast amounts of money on new furnishings throughout, replacement central heating, etc, I would concentrate of staff training. I'd initiate a regular programme and spend time talking to them all, discussing their work and explaining how to behave. Take Aileen, for example.' Mr McCrimmon sat back and listened. 'She's a nice girl, but she hasn't a clue how to serve at table. She never writes down orders and then she forgets half of them. Guests become annoyed.' Zee sighed. 'And that hair!'

Mr McCrimmon raised his eyes to the ceiling in mutual despair.

'It was a disaster area before,' she continued, 'long and straggly, but now that it's bright pink it's totally out of keeping. And she will flick it back over her shoulder when she's dishing out. It's so unhygienic.'

The manager nodded. Zee remembered her confrontation upstairs and decided to pass on Mr Jensen's comments. After all, they *did* make sense.

'Molly and Agnes should work separately and without the accompaniment of the radio. That way they would be through in a quarter of the time, and then they could give a hand in the kitchen. That would ease matters for Mrs Weir and speed service in the dining-room.' Her thoughts stayed with the inquisitive stranger. 'Did Mr Edgar mention anything about a take-over?'

Mr McCrimmon pricked up his ears. 'No. Why?'

Mr Jensen, one of the guests, seems inordinately curious about Greenan Towers. He's constantly taking notes, and earlier this morning he was quizzing me about the size of the grounds'.'

'That's strange.'

Zee pursed her lips. 'I'm convinced I've seen him somewhere before, probably in London.'

'At the Ecrepoint?'

'Possibly.'

Lorn Jensen was exactly the kind of guest such a luxury hotel attracted. Zee had become astute at classifying people, and had marked him down as a businessman—a highly successful one, despite his age, which she guessed to be mid-thirties. The expensive car, solid gold cigarette case and well-tailored suits proved his wealth. Also the authoritative manner told her that he was top dog, and expected to be treated as such, not suffering fools gladly. In little more than a day he had assessed Greenan Towers and already recognised improvements. He would be keenly intelligent and ruthless.

'I wouldn't like to be around if he was taking over,' she said with a wry smile. It was easy to imagine what would happen. Old Jimmy would be given his marching orders and doubtless the rest of the staff would follow him in swift succession.

Mr McCrimmon was involved in his own train of thought. 'If Mr Edgar should appear before Heather leaves to have her baby, would you mind telling him you work in the kitchen?' he asked.

Zee stared at him. 'I beg your pardon?'

'When I engaged you in September I thought Heather would be giving up work within a week or two,' he explained, shifting his bulk in the chair. 'But then she asked if she could stay on until nearer the time the baby was due. I didn't like to refuse. It was impossible to have two receptionists on the books, so I listed you as an extra kitchen hand. I knew that would never be queried.'

Her green eyes opened wider.

'It'll be all right once Heather leaves,' he said hurriedly in an attempt to reassure her. 'Then you'll be classified as a receptionist and it will all be above board.'

'So if the Chairman arrives unexpectedly I hightail it to the kitchen?' she asked with a grin.

'Grab an apron and pretend to be doing something Cordon Bleu-ish with Mrs Weir,' he joked.

'Okay, but talking of Mrs Weir, why does she prepare such a limited choice of food? The same dishes are served up week in, week out. She's an excellent cook, but there's little variety.'

'I've never liked to interfere,' he confessed sheepishly. 'She's a very strong-minded woman.'

What Mr McCrimmon meant was that he was afraid of her, Zee acknowledged with a secret smile. True enough, the bustling Scotswoman possessed a sharp tongue, but Zee was sure that if the suggestion was made she could be persuaded to broaden the scope of her undoubted culinary skills.

'Why don't you write out a list of improvements for me?' the manager prompted, lacing his fingers on the top of his head. 'Perhaps we could make a start on staff training next week.'

Next week! she thought despairingly. Next week equalled never in Mr McCrimmon's language. That fact had come through loud and clear within days of her taking the job at Greenan Towers. At first his lackadaisical manner had frustrated her so much she felt like screaming, but gradually she had been forced to accept that he would never change. He was set like concrete in his ways, and attempts to motivate him would be as productive as banging your head against a brick wall. Now, whenever his sluggish pace annoyed her, she comforted herself with the thought that soon she would be leaving Scotland and returning to London. Her position at the hotel was temporary. She would stay only until Heather had given birth and had returned to work, which promised to be late January, and then they wouldn't see her heels for dust.

'My mother will look after the baby most days,' Heather had told her, 'and I thought I'd ask Mr McCrimmon if I could park the pram in the garden now and then, if Mum's busy.'

Visions of Heather changing nappies on the reception counter had whizzed through Zee's head, but she had merely nodded. By then she would have found a more challenging post in the city, back among professionals, her own kind.

Reluctantly Mr McCrimmon lifted the topmost letter from his wire basket. 'I suppose we'd better make a start.' He paused. 'Would it be possible for you to come in this evening and give a hand in the dining-room? Agnes is usually on duty, but her wee boy's sick and she's asked me for time off.'

'No problem, I'll be there,' she promised.

He gave a smile of gratitude. 'Finish around three

this afternoon, and come back early evening. With luck you should be clear by ten.'

He dictated in fits and starts, and as the pauses between sentences lengthened Zee's mind began to wander. An evening's work at the hotel was perfect. It would give Carol and Struan some time on their own. She had been living with her sister and brother-in-law for the past two months—at their suggestion, she comforted herself, but even so at times she sensed that her presence inhibited them, Struan in particular. It was inevitable. Their three-way relationship was excellent, but when all was said and done she was still an intruder.

Promptly at three she shrugged on her dark brown cape-coat and pushed her fingers into leather gloves. The half dozen letters had been typed and signed. Gathering the envelopes in her fist, she smiled goodbye to Heather who was checking through a vast pile of invoices. The Chairman's telephone call had managed to stir Mr McCrimmon into action, and when Zee had collected the signed mail from his office she had found him on his knees, emptying out the bottom drawer of the filing cabinet. Work had started on compiling the required information.

'It's a wild day,' Heather remarked, glancing out of the window. A gusty wind was whipping the few remaining leaves from the trees, sending them scurrying across the flagged expanse of the courtyard.

Zee nodded, checking her watch. 'With luck I should catch the three-ten bus.'

'Don't you have a hat?' Heather asked. 'Your ears will freeze!'

'I'll manage.'

But as soon as the revolving door deposited her outside, the chill wind made an assault, snatching at wisps of rich red hair and flicking them into her eyes. Zee bent her head, brushing the strands aside before pulling her collar closer. Head down against the force of the wind, she moved forward. There were three steps from the porch. Zee ran down them and thudded straight into a large masculine figure snuggly clad in a tan sheepskin coat.

'Oh!' she gasped as they collided. The impact winded her. Automatically she raised her hands, spreading her fingers across the width of the man's chest in an attempt to steady herself. The wind pounced on the letters held loosely in her grasp and tossed them away.

'Oh!' she said again as the white envelopes were hurled across the flagstones. In dismay she watched them scatter, then gathering her wits gave chase, dimly aware that the man in the sheepskin coat was helping her. It was a short sharp pursuit, but between them they managed to retrieve all six.

'Thanks,' she panted, her cheeks flushed, as he handed her the recalcitrant envelopes. Raising thick lashes, she stared up into ice-blue eyes. Her assistant had been Mr Jensen, his chest rising and falling from the abrupt frantic chase.

'You should have had an elastic band around those,' he said, catching his breath.

Zee bristled. In his opinion all she was fit for was standing in a corner wearing a dunce's cap. She swallowed down her temper.

'Yes, sir,' she said.

He raked aside the fair hair which the wind was slashing across his brow. 'Are you off to the post?' His breathing was becoming steadier.

She resented the question. This stranger was too inquisitive by far. 'Yes,' she returned through her teeth, 'and then I'm going home.'

Ostentatiously he pulled aside the heavy cuff of his jacket and inspected his watch. 'But it's only three.'

The comment was an outright accusation. There were sparks of green fire in Zee's eyes as she swung to face him. God! but he was obnoxious, looking so virtuous and impregnable as he towered over her.

'So what?' she flared, unable to resist retaliation. What right had he to question her actions?

His censorious expression hardened. 'The pregnant girl told me you worked nine until five,' he said sternly.

'Then I'm sneaking off early, aren't I?' she snapped. Let him think what he likes, she fumed, rebellion burning within her as she marched away. When she reached the stone gateposts at the end of the short drive she looked at her wristwatch. Damn him, he had delayed her. With quickening strides she ran down the road and around the corner towards the bus stop. She was too late. In the distance was the three-ten, speeding away at a rate of knots. The bus service was infrequent, now there was only one thing left to do—walk.

Her feet were sore and her hair like a cat-o'-nine-tails by the time she arrived at the house. There had been flurries of rain in the cold wind, battering her unmercifully. It was all that Mr Jensen's fault, she thought caustically. He's trouble with a capital T. Fitting her key into the front door, she let herself in. The house was unusually quiet, the children must be asleep.

'Carol?' she called softly as she removed her coat and gloves, and tried to tidy her hair.

'Up here.' Carol, her younger sister, appeared white-faced on the landing, nine-month-old Gordie balanced on her hip.

'What's the matter?' Zee asked anxiously, noticing the girl's strained expression.

'I've been nauseous all day,' Carol complained. 'It's supposed to be morning sickness, but with me it seems perpetual. I feel dreadful!' Twin tears rolled down her cheeks. 'And this monster has done nothing but yell.' She cast a bitter glance at the plump baby gurgling in her grasp. 'He's driving me mad!'

Zee ran up the stairs. 'I'll take him,' she offered. Her nephew raised his arms and hurled himself towards her. She cuddled him close as Carol smiled a weak thank you.

'Where's Emma?' Zee asked.

'Asleep, thank goodness. She was at play-group this

morning, and that always tires her out.' Noisily Carol
blew her nose. 'The trouble is, she won't sleep tonight.'

Slipping a comforting arm around her sister's
shoulders, Zee guided her into the bedroom. 'You have
a rest,' she said. 'I'll look after Gordie, and Emma when
she wakes up.'

Carol sank down gratefully and pulled the eiderdown
up to her chin. 'You're a gem, Zee,' she smiled, but
suddenly she raised her head. 'Why are you home so
early?'

'Mr McCrimmon asked if I would work this evening.
I must be back at Greenan Towers by seven.' Zee
paused on her way out of the door. 'You try to sleep
now. I'll feed the kids and get my own dinner.'

'Struan'll be in at five,' Carol murmured, already half
asleep. 'He'll help.'

It was nearer six when her brother-in-law arrived
home, and by then Zee had bathed and fed both
children. They sat on either side of her on the settee,
pink and shining in their clean pyjamas as she read
them a story. In response to Struan's cheery shout she
picked up Gordie, and followed two-year-old Emma
into the kitchen to greet him.

'There,' he gave a smile of satisfaction as he slid a
large cardboard box of groceries onto the work surface.
'That'll save Carol's legs.'

Zee smiled at her dark-haired brother-in-law. 'You're
very considerate.'

He brushed the tribute aside with a careless wave of
his hand. 'It's hard for her, having to struggle on the
bus with two small kids and a pushchair. I hope that by
next year we'll be able to afford a second car.' He
glanced round. 'Where is she?'

Zee pulled a face. 'She's been feeling rotten again.'

'Oh dear!' He gave a sigh of commiseration and bent
to lift the clamouring Emma, flicking his daughter's soft
curls with the tip of his finger. 'Still, it won't last for
ever.'

There was the sound of footsteps on the stairs and

Carol walked in. 'No, it won't,' she agreed with a laugh. Her face was happy again and her eyes were shining. 'I feel much better now, thanks to Zee.' She gave her a dazzling smile. Gordie held out his arms. 'And who's the most beautiful baby in the world?' she cooed, taking him from Zee and giving him an affectionate squeeze.

'A couple of hours ago you said he was a monster.' Zee watched as the baby tugged at her sister's silken fringe.

'I've changed my mind.'

'You're always changing your mind,' she accused, half laughing.

Struan let out a bellow of disbelief. 'Good God, listen who's talking! Since when were you a paragon of constancy, Miss Robertson? I've never met a more volatile pair than you and Carol. It's a toss-up who's the worst.'

'Don't exaggerate,' his wife intervened hotly. 'I *am* consistent. All I've ever wanted to do was get married and raise a family.'

'That's true,' he conceded, 'but you must admit you do tend to plunge from elation to despair in three seconds flat.'

'Because I'm pregnant!'

'Okay, I'll give you the benefit of the doubt.' He swung to Zee. 'But what's your excuse, ladybird?'

She put her hands on her hips and glared at him. 'I'm not moody.'

'You're not,' he agreed, his dark eyes sparkling in amusement at her belligerent stance. 'But you must admit you're bloody impetuous! Look at your behaviour with Mike, the poor devil didn't know whether he was coming or going. One minute there were wedding bells in the air, the next you were flouncing away, hurling abuse over your shoulder.'

'I wasn't. We weren't suited, that's all,' she said stiffly.

He set Emma down on the floor and rested back against the worktop. 'What you mean is *you* decided he didn't suit *you*. As far as I can remember he didn't have time to draw breath.'

Carol slipped her arm through Struan's. 'You didn't give it much of a try, Zee. Did you?'

She glowered at the pair of them. What right had they to gang up on her?

'It doesn't take long to discover when something isn't going to work,' she retorted, her cheeks growing pink. 'My experience with Mike was useful, it strengthened my convictions—that it's impossible for a woman to combine marriage with a career.'

'So marriage is taboo?' Carol jeered.

'For the time being, yes. I intend to devote the next few years to my career. If I do marry it will be when I'm firmly established in the hotel business. My husband will know exactly what he's taking on. He'll accept that my work is as important as his, if not *more* important.'

Struan exploded into another guffaw. 'Poppycock! No man worth his salt would be prepared to tag along as a sidekick. You want a mouse, not a man.'

Her chin lifted. 'No, I don't.'

He raised his eyebrows and grinned. 'Well, that's all you'll get, ladybird. However,' he rubbed his hands together, 'shall we agree to differ? You two girls grab a sherry and take the kids into the lounge. I'll rustle up some food to prove I'm not completely chauvinistic.'

Carol kissed his cheek. 'You're a pet,' she said.

'Struan really is marvellous,' Zee commented when she and Carol were settled before the fire. A delicious aroma of grilling steak was beginning to drift from the kitchen and they could hear him whistling as he prepared the meal.

'He's one in a million,' her sister agreed, casting Zee a sidelong glance. 'Did Mike never help with the cooking?'

Zee hitched Emma closer on to her lap. 'Never. He decided he was on to a cushy number when he moved into the flat.'

'Didn't the landlord object to a man sharing with two girls? It seems an odd arrangement to me.'

She shook her head. 'No. Mixed flatting is quite common in London these days. It was supposed to be platonic, of course. We each had a separate bedroom.'

'But it didn't stay platonic?'

'No,' Zee said impatiently. 'It wasn't long before he came sneaking into my room in the middle of the night.'

Carol arched a brow. 'But you didn't turn him away?'

'I didn't have much option—besides, I thought I loved him. We were intending to be married. He was tall and dark and handsome, and very strong, definitely the pick of the crop at the Ecrepoint.'

'An up-and-coming executive?'

'Absolutely. Destined to go to the top with all his charm,' Zee remarked drily. 'Everybody liked him. Irate guests were always steered to Mike to pacify. He worked wonders, within minutes they were eating out of his hand.'

Carol sipped her sherry. 'Sounds like the answer to a maiden's prayer.'

'Except that what he really required was a maid, not a maiden,' came the pithy reply. She had never told her sister the full story about Mike, and had no intention of doing so now. The less Carol knew, the better.

'You were too hard on him,' Carol protested. 'You can't blame him for showing a blind spot where the cooking was concerned when he had two female flatmates.'

'And a blind spot for washing up and cleaning and doing the laundry? On reflection, he spent most of his spare time under the car or playing rugby.'

'Or making love?' There was a glint in Carol's eye.

'Or *trying* to make love,' Zee conceded tightly.

'But living with him in a flat with another girl wasn't a true indication of what married life would have been like.'

Zee sighed at her sister's persistence. 'Mike and I had

had long discussions on equality. He had agreed that my career was as worthwhile as his, but it quickly became apparent that if we were married I'd be expected to wait on him hand and foot.' And there were other reasons for leaving him, she added silently, private reasons . . .

'So you walked out!'

'Yes!'

Emma nestled closer against Zee's chest, sucking wetly at her thumb.

'From now on I shall be footloose and fancy free. I have no intention of becoming seriously involved with a man for a very long time.'

'Grub's up, girls!' Struan shouted from the kitchen.

After dinner Zee washed her face and re-did her make-up, then clipped back her heavy hair with two tortoiseshell combs. Flinging on her coat, she ran down the stairs.

'I'll drive you round in the car,' Struan offered. 'It's a cold wet night, so I'll collect you when you're finished.'

She smiled gratefully. 'If you could arrange to be cloned, Struan, I just might be tempted to marry the other one, career or no career.'

'Good idea,' Carol beamed as she came into the hall to join them, a sleeping Gordie in her arms. 'I'd like to see you settled.'

Zee gave a dramatic sigh. 'Here we go again! Another lecture from little sister on how miserable I shall be if I'm left on the shelf, and that I'm twenty-five and time is passing by, so why don't I find myself a good man, smartish.' She laughed. 'All you married people are the same, you want everyone to disappear into the pit with you.'

'It's not a pit,' Carol protested.

Zee raised an eyebrow. 'Be honest—at times you'd give your eye-teeth to be free, like me.' She turned towards the front door, but as she shoved her hands into her pockets, her face fell. Retrieving the six envelopes she held them up. 'Oh dear, I've forgotten to post these. Could we stop at a letter box?' She frowned. 'It's all that Jensen man's fault.'

'Who's he?' Struan asked.

Zee wrinkled her nose. 'He's an interfering, bad-tempered giant, whom I would personally be delighted to toss from the highest turret of Greenan Towers.'

'Sounds to have made quite an impression,' he laughed, collecting his car keys from the hall table.

'How old is he?' Carol asked, alert all of a sudden.

'Mid-thirties.' Zee shook her head. 'Oh, no, take that gleam out of your eyes.' She turned to Struan. 'Every time I mention a male anywhere between fifteen and fifty, Carol jots him down as a prospective husband.' She swivelled to confront her sister. 'Well, this time it's one hundred per cent no-go. Lorn Jensen is unbearable. The sooner he disappears from my breathing space, the better!'

CHAPTER TWO

GOLDEN light filtered through the latticed windows as Struan deposited Zee at the hotel.

'I'll be back around ten-fifteen,' he promised before driving away.

The wind had dropped and for the present the night sky was clear, though ominous rain clouds hung high above the sea, to the west. Stars twinkled above and the silvery crescent of a waning moon bathed the rambling hotel in pale shimmering light. Zee could understand why the previous Chairman of the Devenay group, Mr Robert, had placed Greenan Towers high in his affection. There was a compelling charm about the solid sandstone building. Her eyes wandered over the collection of mock battlements and turreted peaks. All wasted space and difficult to cope with internally, of course, but aesthetically it was a fascinating spread of architecture, half covered as it was with sprawling dark green ivy.

By eight-thirty most of the tables in the high-ceilinged dining-room were occupied. Only a handful of guests were staying at the hotel, but Mrs Weir's good cooking attracted a regular clientele of local people. There was no sign of the sour-tempered Mr Jensen. Perhaps he's dining out, Zee pondered, her eyes flicking over the tables. Aileen was occupied at the gigantic mahogany sideboard at one side of the room where cutlery, crockery and napkins were stored, while Molly busied herself with the dessert trolley. Ceiling-to-floor crimson velvet curtains had been drawn across two bay windows, shutting out the cold November night, but even their rich softness was unable to create a cosy atmosphere. The dining-room lacked character. Its proportions were too grand for intimacy and the

29

furniture too nondescript to grace it with an air of elegance.

Everything was running smoothly. Zee felt much more at ease without the forbidding presence of Mr Jensen. To relieve Aileen and Molly she had been serving drinks and taking orders, being careful to write them down. In consequence there had been no irate enquiries for missing courses. No one had been kept waiting, indeed the service had been swiftly efficient. Now there was a lull, and she used the time to slip behind the semi-circular bar in the corner of the room and restore order. Screwing the cap on to a bottle of whisky, she reached across to slide it into its allotted place on the glass shelf behind her. The bar wall was mirrored and as she stretched a reflected movement caught her eye. Her stomach plunged. Mr Jensen, immaculate in a navy pin-striped suit and pale blue shirt, was coming through the door. He hesitated for a moment, frowning impatiently.

Zee abandoned the bar and hurried over. 'Good evening, sir.' A welcoming smile was dredged up. As usual his expression was stern and she guessed he would be alert to the slightest fault. Already tension was tightening in her throat. He would pounce soon, she knew. Leading him to his table, she noticed lines of strain scoring the tight skin around his eyes. He looked tired, and as he sank down in the chair he rubbed a weary hand across his brow.

'Would you care for a drink, sir?' she asked, trying to sound cool and efficient.

'Not yet, thanks. I'll have a look at the menu first. I'm famished.'

'The sea air must have given you an appetite.' Her reply was tart—too tart, she realised, for he glanced up suspiciously, subjecting her to a piercing examination. She stayed poker-faced, returning his look with a steady one of her own. How far dare I go before he explodes? she wondered. Not too far, that was true. She would have to tread carefully, and yet she itched to give this superior being his comeuppance. According to reports he had spent the late afternoon and early evening striding around Greenan Towers until everyone was feeling suicidal.

He ordered minestrone soup from the menu, followed by steak and kidney pie. 'Do you have broccoli?' he asked laconically.

'I'll enquire, sir.' She knew all too well Mrs Weir served only carrots, peas and cauliflower and suspected Mr Jensen had also worked that out. He was too damn clever. The request was a challenge, she knew it, and he knew it. If I had a bicycle I would ride round to Carol's house, and commandeer the broccoli I know she has in the fridge, Zee thought, irritation thinning her mouth.

'Sorry, lassie, no broccoli,' Mrs Weir said predictably when she went into the kitchen. 'Is it for that fair fellow?'

She nodded.

'He's a wee villain, that one,' the cook pronounced crossly, ladling out the soup. 'Yesterday he demanded spinach, and at lunchtime he asked for artichokes. Any more odd requests from him and I'll go out there and give him a piece of my mind. Artichokes indeed!' she muttered. 'What does he think this place is, the pick of the Michelin Guide?'

Swallowing her pride, Zee placed the soup bowl on a tray and returned to the dining-room. 'Sorry, sir, no broccoli this evening,' she said, striving to give the impression that ninety-nine times out of a hundred it *was* on the menu, and that he had merely been unlucky. Carefully avoiding his eyes, she set down the soup. 'However, we do have . . .'

'Don't tell me, I know,' he taunted. 'Carrots, peas or cauliflower.' He flashed her a smug look of triumph which she ignored. 'I'll take carrots and cauliflower, please, and make sure they're fresh.'

'Yes, sir.'

His final words had been barked out and she would have clicked her heels and given a mock salute if she had dared. But she didn't. Quelling her temper, she passed the order to Aileen and returned to the bar. Several customers had glasses to be replenished and she was kept busy, mixing cocktails and filling beer tankards. From the corner of her eye she was aware of Aileen removing Mr Jensen's empty soup bowl and arriving with his main course. As the girl served the pie, she tossed back a lank pink strand from her shoulder. He winced visibly. He was studying the outrageous hair with something approaching horror and as Aileen completed dishing out his vegetables he said something to her.

Another complaint. Tensely Zee waited for Aileen to burst into floods of tears, for the multi-coloured hair had been provoking comments all evening.

'Nobody likes it, they think I look strange,' Aileen had whispered, chewing her lip. 'Perhaps I should wash the colour out. Everyone's treating it as a joke.' Her chin had trembled and Zee had realised she was on the verge of tears. All it needed was one more barbed comment and the teenager would go to pieces. One thing was certain, Mr Jensen would not treat the pink hair as a joke. He would consider it a personal insult. But much to her surprise Aileen merely gave a half-hearted smile and scuttled away towards the kitchen. Most of the diners had finished their meals and were now at the aperitif stage, so Zee was occupied, threading her way backwards and forwards between the tables. On several occasions she was forced to pass Mr Jensen and each time he raised his head and glowered at her. What's wrong now? she wondered, for he was becoming impatient, drumming his fingers on the tablecloth. When she returned to the bar, Aileen was waiting.

'Could you have a word with Mr Jensen?' she pleaded, large dark eyes anxious in her white face. 'He asked me for something when I was serving dinner, but I must have heard wrong. I thought he said he wanted a screwdriver, and I've been trying to work out what he means.' She put her head on one side. 'That can't be right, can it? Please could you ask him what he meant? I daren't go back, he'd skin me alive.' Fearfully she glanced across. 'He frightens me.'

'A screwdriver is a drink—vodka and orange,' Zee explained with a smile.

'Is it?' Aileen looked astonished.

'I'll make one up and take it to him. Don't worry,' she said, patting the girl's arm. Swiftly she mixed the drink and carried it over on a tray. 'Your Screwdriver, sir.'

'And about time, too.' He took a swift gulp.

'There was a mix-up,' she explained gaily in a desperate attempt to smooth his ruffled feathers. 'Aileen didn't understand. She thought you meant a real screwdriver, a tool.' She forced a laugh, but his frosty glare excluded any agreement that the mistake contained the remotest hint of comedy.

'Why didn't she ask what I meant if she didn't understand?' he demanded. 'It seems the logical thing to do.'

Zee's blood began to boil. The words were flung out before she could stop herself. 'Because she's terrified of you, that's why. You reduce her to a quivering mass.'

'And how about you, Miss Robertson?' A sardonic brow arched. 'Do I reduce you to a quivering mass, too?'

'Like hell!' she retorted, spinning away, her face in flames. Damn, she thought, her pulses racing, I've gone too far. He'll complain to Mr McCrimmon that I was impolite, and I was. But he deserved it. With shaking hands she rinsed out used glasses and concentrated on tending the bar, trying to take no notice of the table at the far end of the room where Mr Jensen was finishing his meal, but it was impossible. She glanced at her watch. Almost a quarter to ten. In another half hour she would be free, free from the arrogant stranger. Although she knew it was purely imagination, there seemed to be a current of electricity sparking across the dining-room, intermittently joining them. Ignoring his presence was beyond her, and she worked, head down, wishing him a thousand miles away.

Gradually the room cleared. It was Wednesday evening and diners were leaving early, ready for a fresh start in the morning. The orders for drinks petered out. Zee wiped and polished the glasses and listed bottles which needed to be replenished. Tomorrow she would collect necessary wines and spirits from the store in the cellar.

'Excuse me.' Mr Jensen was clicking his fingers at her as though she was a pet poodle. Pinning on a composed expression, she approached, convinced he was preparing to mete out some harsh reprimand.

'Would you care for another drink, sir?' she asked guardedly, her temples throbbing with apprehension.

'A brandy, and please have one yourself.'

Zee almost dropped her order pad in astonishment. He actually sounded pleasant! Narrowing her eyes, she studied him for a long moment, her mind working overtime. What was the snag? What was coming next? His face gave nothing away. Perhaps her heated accusation had made him stop and think. Perhaps now he would apologise for his brusque behaviour. She opened her mouth to speak, but he was there first.

'That young waitress should be banned from the hotel until she does something about her disgraceful hair,' he growled, leaning back in his chair, and taking his cigarette case from an inside pocket.

All Zee's previous feelings of dislike clicked smartly back into place. 'I'll bring you your drink, sir,' she said, passing over his comment about Aileen. 'I won't have one myself.' Although it was hard to say, she added, 'thank you.'

Seething, she poured his brandy. If it had been possible, she would have gladly laced it with cyanide. Back to his table she went.

'It beats me why anyone chooses to stay in this

dump,' he remarked, as she set the drink down before him.

'*You're* here, sir,' she responded pointedly, glaring at him.

He pulled long and slow on his cigarette, frowning against the smoke. 'That's different.' Idly he glanced around the deserted room. Aileen and Molly were clearing tables, coming and going between the kitchen. 'I must admit the food is good,' he commented, but it was with reluctance.

Zee's tone was hotly positive. 'The food is *excellent*!'

'It would be more exciting if there was greater variety. I suspect steak and kidney pie has appeared on the menu every Wednesday evening, without fail, for the past ten years.' As usual his suspicion was not far off the mark.

'I've really no idea, sir,' she said witheringly.

Looking directly into her eyes, he smiled, amused by her impudence. The change in his face was startling. A deep groove appeared in one tanned cheek. Good heavens, he has a dimple! she thought. If Robbie Burns had leapt down from his plinth in Burns' Statue Square and given her a hug, she couldn't have been more surprised. The transformation took her unawares and unconsciously she smiled back.

'To some degree catering profits must subsidise the lack of paying guests,' he continued. Pulling out a chair at his table, he motioned her towards it. 'Can you spare a few minutes?'

'Well . . .' she hesitated. The dimple had indicated that somewhere, beyond that wall of criticism, was a human being. Be wise, Zee, she told herself. The smart ploy would be to accept the invitation and disarm him with friendliness. If he could be persuaded to regard Greenan Towers' faults with a benevolent eye, life would be much easier for everyone. She glanced round. The dining-room was empty. Even Molly and Aileen had finished for the night. With a tentative smile she sat down beside him.

'Are you sure you won't have a drink?' he asked pleasantly.

'No, thanks.' Surface conviviality was all she was prepared to offer. She had no wish to become beholden to him, even for the price of a drink. 'The hotel is usually fully booked on racing weekends,' she said defensively, watching his long tanned fingers as he tapped ash from his cigarette. Golden hair shone on the back of his hands.

'And how frequent are they held?'

'Roughly once a month throughout the year.' Raising a shapely brow, Zee gave him a calculating look. 'You seem very interested in Greenan Towers.'

'General curiosity,' he replied, exhaling a waft of grey smoke.

She did not believe him.

'Why are you staying here?' she asked.

A shadow crossed his eyes. 'I'm enjoying the sea air,' he said, deadpan.

'I see.' But she didn't.

'There weren't many guests during this past summer,' he drawled.

So he had been examining the register, too. Holding back a tight comment on his inquisitiveness, Zee shrugged. Confirmation was unnecessary. Obviously all the facts were at his fingertips.

Intelligent blue eyes travelled across the cumbersome high-backed chair, the old-fashioned tables which were so heavy to move, the scratched sideboard. 'The whole place needs to be ripped out and completely modernised.' Jettisoning his cigarette, he turned to face her. 'Doesn't it?' he demanded.

There was a tinge of accusation which unsettled her and Zee leapt to the defence. 'The Devenay family like it as it is. They don't want this hotel to be changed,' she announced dramatically.

'Oh no?' There was a sarcastic twitch to the corner of his mouth.

'*No.* Mr Robert, father of the present Chairman,

spent his holidays here when he was a child. He liked things the way they are,' she explained. 'Or perhaps I should say the way they *were*.'

'Were,' he agreed, 'but times change.' He fidgeted with the almost empty glass on the table. 'Tell me more about this Mr Robert.'

Zee caught her full lower lip in her teeth. There was a new intensity in his expression that intrigued her. 'I don't know much,' she confessed. 'There are some photographs of him in the reception area.'

'I hadn't noticed,' he said briefly.

'They're behind the desk,' she explained, surprised that something had actually managed to escape his all-seeing eye. 'Mr Robert was an amateur jockey in his youth. The pictures show him receiving trophies at various meets. If you want more information you could always ask Mr McCrimmon, he knew him.'

'I'm not interested,' he assured her, carelessly twisting the glass round and round on the white damask tablecloth.

I don't believe you, she thought. Something doesn't add up here. She decided to test him. 'Mr Robert has three children,' she said. A strange emotion flickered across his face, confirming her suspicions. 'Mr Edgar, the present Chairman, and two girls,'

'I know.' His voice was flat.

'You do?' Surprise lifted her words. 'How?'

He made a vague gesture with his hand. 'I can't remember. Probably I read it in a newspaper somewhere.'

Zee thought the possibility unlikely.

He stared into his glass. 'I follow the stock market, taking a particular interest in hotel shares. From time to time there have been articles about the Devenay chain in the financial papers.'

'I see.' But his explanation left her unconvinced.

He swallowed down the last mouthful of his drink. 'If Greenan Towers was mine I'd offload it pretty damn quick.'

At least he was not a prospective buyer, she decided with relief. 'But what about the staff?' she asked, resenting the pitilessly impersonal attitude. 'Several of them have worked here all their lives.'

As she spoke a terrifying thought struck her. Perhaps he was an asset stripper, buying up failing businesses for a song. Anything of value would be commandeered, he would dismiss the employees outright, and demolish the building before finally selling the land for an exorbitant figure. She had heard of men like that. Men who were ruthless, profit their only concern.

'It strikes me the staff would benefit from a change,' he said drily.

'They're not that bad,' Zee declared, feline eyes flashing.

'You're the only decent one among them,' he told her.

If it was a compliment it didn't sound like one. Pell-mell she rushed to their defence. 'They try their best!'

'Well, it isn't good enough,' he threw back. 'If that damn waitress tosses her hair over my plate just one more time, I swear I shall grab the scissors and shear her clean, like a sheep.'

For a transitory moment Zee wondered if he was joking. He wasn't. The savage look in his eyes told her that.

'You're attractive and well groomed,' he continued, flicking an expert eye over her shapely figure in the tailored silk suit. 'Why don't you teach her how to smarten up her appearance?'

'Because it's none of my business. I only work here,' she retorted.

'You could use tact and diplomacy to take out the sting,' he instructed righteously.

Openmouthed, she stared at him. If he had employed a little tact and diplomacy himself he would have found everyone at Greenan Towers far more relaxed and helpful. Instead his critical manner had turned Aileen into a nervous wreck, alienated Mrs Weir, and filled Zee herself with a furious desire to chop him down to size. She was about to fling back a scathing comment on his own attitude when the dining-room opened. It was Struan. With a sense of relief she rose to greet him. What was the point in losing her temper? The arrogant Mr Jensen followed no dictates but his own. 'Thanks for coming,' she said, hurrying towards her brother-in-law. Her smile was extra bright, beaming out gratitude at his unknowing rescue. The conversation had been becoming a little too fraught. Struan put his arm around her and grinned.

Scraping back his chair, Mr Jensen joined them at the door. 'I suppose I'd better go now.' His eyes were on Struan, assessing him.

Zee checked her watch. 'The bar's closed, sir, but tea or coffee are available in the lounge. Just ring the bell for service.'

'How about hot Bovril?' he challenged. There was a teasing flash of the dimple, but before she could reply his humour faded, and she noticed again how tired he looked.

He yawned. 'I'm off to bed.'

'Goodnight, sir,' she said demurely.

'Get your coat, ladybird,' Struan instructed as they moved into the wide entrance hall. They were laughing together as Zee buttoned up her coat.

Mr McCrimmon emerged from the office at the end of the hall. Looking somewhat dazed, he rubbed the back of his neck with a heavy hand as he called to Zee. 'Could you work tomorrow evening? Come in from nine until lunchtime, have the afternoon free, and then help out in the dining-room again?'

She nodded. 'No problem.'

'Thanks.' Tiredly he stretched his arms. 'I've made a start on that financial report, but it's hard going.' He shook his head, a bemused expression on his lined face. 'I hope Mr Edgar doesn't start pressing for it.'

But in the morning there was a follow-up telephone call from the Chairman's London office. Zee spent all her time jotting down rough notes, locating invoices, typing out tentative columns which Mr McCrimmon inevitably changed as fresh snippets of evidence were unearthed. She had always enjoyed working under pressure and coped happily but soon realised that the manager was in danger of cracking up. He had never been stretched before, and he wandered unhappily around his office, mislaying vital information, forgetfully switching from one topic to another, and sinking into a trough of frantic desperation.

It was a relief when her morning stint was finished and a free afternoon, away from the tensions of the hotel, stretched before her. Though doubtless, she thought, as she ate her lunch in Carol's kitchen, by tomorrow morning all the sheets she had prepared would be scored out and require typing again. She thanked her lucky stars she had had the foresight to enrol for a brief secretarial course after her four years at university and could type adequately, though at a low speed.

'I'll take Emma for a walk,' she suggested, as she cleared the table. Carol was looking peaky again. Already she had made a couple of rushed trips to the bathroom. 'Gordie's down for his nap, so you try and sleep,' Zee continued.

'Thanks, I'll return the favour some time,' said Carol, as she clung, waxen-faced, to the stair-post.

'Not for years and years, I hope.' Zee zipped up Emma's pink and white anorak, tucking her baby curls into the hood.

When she had fastened the little girl into her pushchair, she set off down the road towards the shore. The weather was still bitterly cold, an icy wind blowing from the sea. Her pace was brisk, and although she was snug in coffee-coloured cords and a white feather-filled jacket, the chill gusts sent occasional shivers dancing along her spine. Within minutes her neatly brushed hair was tossed into disarray, and she laughingly accepted defeat as it swirled around her head. It was invigorating to be in the fresh air. When they reached the dunes she lifted Emma out and together they wandered along, Zee dragging the pushchair behind her through the sand. The shore was almost deserted. In the distance one or two people were walking their dogs and a solitary horse and rider cantered by. To her far right was the estuary of the River Doon.

'Look at the birds, Emma,' she said, bending down and pointing out seagulls and diving cormorants, but Emma's interest lay elsewhere.

'Find shells,' she instructed.

Parking the pushchair on the crest of a dune, Zee took her niece by the hand and walked down to the edge of the sea.

'There's plenty here, look.' She pointed out thousands of small white shells embedded in the hardpacked sand. Emma dropped to her haunches, and began poking around.

Suddenly there was an extra fierce gust of wind. The canopy of the pushchair filled with air and it began to roll down the sandhill, in slow motion. Zee turned back to catch it, but at that moment Emma let out a bloodcurdling scream. She had plopped down on her bottom, marooning herself in the centre of a shallow pool left by the tide. For a split second Zee didn't know which way to turn. Teetering on the dune's brink, the pushchair was poised to tumble on to a patch of stones which could cause it to buckle. On the other hand her niece was yelling blue murder. The choice had to be Emma. Running down the beach, she rescued the toddler from the water, scooping her up into her arms. Breathing heavily, she pivoted to assess the damage to the pushchair, but to her amazement it was safe and sound, still on top of the sand-dune, held in the capable hands of Mr Jensen.

'Thanks very much,' she said, hurrying up the narrow strip of beach.

Lifting the pushchair in one big hand, he brought it down to her on the sand. Zee mopped up Emma's soaking padded trousers with a spare nappy she discovered in the pushchair pocket.

'Find shells, Zee. Shells, Zee,' Emma demanded, none the worse for her wetting. She toddled happily away.

Mr Jensen nodded down at the pushchair. 'I'll look after this while you keep an eye on that young lady,' he offered.

'Thank you,' said Zee. 'Are you out for a walk?'

'I'm having some of that sea air to give me an appetite,' he teased with a grin. The elusive dimple appeared and stayed there. He was smiling at her quite foolishly, and Zee smiled back. Good humour suited him. Heather had been right, he *was* attractive, but only when he smiled.

'I owe you an apology,' he said, as they began to follow Emma along the shore. 'It was wrong of me to question the time you left the hotel yesterday afternoon. I hadn't realised you worked in the evenings.'

'You shouldn't jump to conclusions, should you?' she retorted, lifting her chin.

'No.' A smile quirked his mouth as he noticed her satisfaction at his apology. 'It's rare that I'm unsure of my facts, but on that occasion I was.'

Zee's green eyes flashed. So it had been a superficial apology at best! 'It must be nice to be perfect,' she commented stiffly, furious at his unrepentance.

'*Almost* perfect,' he adjusted with a grin.

'Hurry up, Zee!' Emma shouted. She had wandered on and now paused, waiting for them to catch up.

'What does Zee stand for?' he asked, blandly ignoring her annoyance, for the question had snapped her onto the alert.

'Aziza,' she supplied warily. She hoped he wasn't about to indulge in another inquisition, but apart from raising his brows at the name's rarity he made no comment. For a few minutes they walked along the beach and she allowed herself to relax. It seemed stupid to remain silent. She had no objection to talking to him, so long as he didn't persist in asking intrusive questions. 'It's a Malay name,' she offered. 'I'm Scots, but I was born in Malaysia. My father managed a rubber plantation south of Kuala Lumpur.'

'It must have been a vastly different kind of life from Bonnie Scotland,' he said, glancing at the wind scoured sandhills and pale grey sky.

'It's much colder here,' Zee gave a shudder. 'When I first started at boarding school in Ayr, and flying back to Malaysia for holidays, I was forever getting confused about what to wear. I used to walk around half dressed here. In the tropics you get by with only a tee-shirt and shorts so it felt odd to be wrapped up against the winter cold in layers and layers of thick clothing.'

'Like the little girl,' he commented, watching Emma as she plonked herself down in the sand in her padded suit and tried to scoop up a shell in her stubby fingers. 'I presume she doesn't belong to you?'

'No, thank goodness,' Zee told him hastily.

'Why "thank goodness"?' he asked. 'She looks like a poppet to me.'

'She is.' The assurance was sincere. 'It's just that I have no desire to get married and have children yet. My sister, Carol, is Emma's mother and she's producing sufficient offspring for the two of us. She's expecting her third.'

'You sound as though you don't approve.' Carefully he watched her profile. Some inner emotion had tightened her lips.

She brushed aside a strand of bright red hair which was clinging to the petal smoothness of her cheek. 'Carol's crazy,' she said in a flat voice. 'She's only twenty-three, but she's tied down already. She'll be in her mid-thirties before she can possibly attempt to revive her career.'

'Perhaps she doesn't want to,' he replied. There was a fierce light in Zee's eyes which made him wonder.

'I don't think she's career-orientated, but that's not the point.'

'Then what is?'

'That once a woman is married and has children, she's virtually locked away from civilisation for the next fifteen years or so.'

'Surely it's not as bad as that!' he laughed.

'It is,' she assured him, pushing her hands into her pockets and scowling at the sea. On the horizon she could pick out the misty blue outline of mountains across the Firth of Clyde. 'Marriage is supposed to be a partnership,' she continued, 'but it's always the woman who is left with the dirty work. *And* she's the one who has to give way all along the line.'

'You have a very one-sided view,' he protested.

'No, I'm realistic.' She stopped in her tracks to face him, emphasising her argument with flamboyant movements of her hands. Zee on her soapbox, as Struan teased. 'Women are shunted around, sometimes being forced to live in a town or a country they hate, just to suit their husbands. They have no choice in the matter. My mother's case was typical.'

'Didn't she like Malaysia?'

'She hated it,' Zee said briefly, then she looked down at the sand and scuffed her toe. 'Sorry, I didn't mean to become so heated.'

'Must be the red hair,' he grinned.

'Maybe.' Her face was serious. 'But marriage is not for me, not for a long time. I'm ambitious. My career comes first.'

'You'll change your mind,' he said as they followed in Emma's wake.

His smug confidence irritated her and she whirled round. 'I will not! I bet you're married. Married people are always inveigling us single folk to take the plunge too. They can't rest until everyone has been marched up the aisle.'

He shook his head, amused by her heated reaction. 'Actually I'm a bachelor, but even so I consider marriage to be an eminently satisfactory institution.'

'Oh, yes?' she taunted. 'Then how come you

haven't tried it?'

'Perhaps I prefer to play the field?' There was a teasing lift of a brow. 'I was engaged to be married once, but it fell through.'

'You developed cold feet?' Zee quizzed, giving him a sidelong glance.

A muscle clenched in his jaw. 'No. My fiancée's family didn't consider I was suitable.' Abruptly he lifted an arm and pointed towards the headland in the distance where a crumbling stone tower clung to the edge of the cliffs. 'What's that?' he asked, changing the subject with ironclad finality.

'Greenan Castle. It's about seven hundred years old. I don't think anyone ever lived there permanently, but it was used in times of conflict as a secure stronghold against attack.'

'It's certainly that,' he agreed. 'Approach from the sea would be impossible.'

As they walked towards the ruin, her mind careered away. Why would anyone consider the virile Mr Jensen unsuitable as a marriage partner? For virile he certainly was, in his tight jeans and pale grey anorak. He was also intelligent, successful at his job, whatever that might be, and, she suspected reluctantly, good fun when it suited him. Now that he was relaxed, he looked younger. The wind flicked a strand of hair into his eyes and he tossed back his head, releasing it. She altered her original assessment. Thirty-two or three, she decided. It was his complaining face which made him look older. In his formal suit, the leashed energy of the wide shoulders, lean hips and long legs had been muted, but now he looked young and strong full of animal magnetism. Why would any woman in her right mind turn him down, if marriage was what they wanted! Inspecting him from beneath curling black lashes, Zee wondered what he would be like as a lover. His nose and jaw were straight, diamond-hard, but the full lips beneath the bristling moustache gave a subtle hint of a more sensual facet of his personality. What would it feel

like to be kissed by a man with a moustache? The only
moustache she had ever come into contact with had
belonged to her Great-Uncle John, and he had been
eighty-three at the time. A chuckle escaped.

'What's the joke?' he asked.

Zee flushed, relieved he was unable to read her
thoughts.

'Nothing.'

Without warning, Emma wearied of the shells. 'Carry
me,' she insisted, screwing up her face in readiness for a
blast of anger if her wishes were not pandered to
immediately. She stood stock still on the sand. Zee
hoisted her up into her arms.

'Can you manage, or shall I take her?' Her
companion paused as she adjusted Emma's hood
to keep out the cold.

'It's okay. She's not heavy, but thanks for the offer,
Mr Jensen.'

'The name's Lorn.'

'Lorn,' she agreed tentatively. 'That's a Scots name.'

'I'm a mongrel,' he revealed, half-smiling. 'My father
was Scots and my mother is Danish.'

'Ah! Heather thought you had Scandinavian blood.'

'Heather's the highly pregnant lady?' he asked, as
they turned to retrace their steps along the shore.

Emma stuck her thumb into her mouth and examined
Lorn in great detail. He winked at her, and made her
giggle.

'Heather is hanging on until the bitter end,' Zee
confirmed. 'I wouldn't be surprised if she gave birth
behind the reception counter.'

'I hope not!' he laughed, sharing her amusement,
then his face stilled. 'Why does her husband allow her
to go out to work at this late stage? She'd be far better
off at home with her feet up.'

'There isn't a husband.'

'Stupid woman,' he said cuttingly. The lighthearted
mood of a moment ago vanished. 'There was a stiffness
in his expression, the blue eyes coldly censorious again.

'It wasn't entirely her fault. Her boy-friend didn't reveal until too late that he was already married,' she protested in an attempt to vindicate her colleague. 'I understand he's trying to get a divorce.'

'In this age of birth control there's no excuse for unwanted children.' Lorn clenched his jaw, the muscles working angrily.

'The baby isn't unwanted,' she returned.

'No?' He gave a grunt of disbelief. 'Even so, it's wildly irresponsible to bring a child into the world without a proper father.'

'Heather will be all right, her parents are willing to help. And eventually I expect her boy-friend will marry her,' Zee retorted. His unexpected fury had caught her off balance, making her feel uncomfortable and on edge again. The distaste with which he viewed Greenan Towers paled beneath this violent condemnation of Heather's unwed motherhood.

'And what about the child?' he demanded, eyes glittering with suppressed emotion. 'Has anyone given a thought to how it will feel, branded with the stigma of illegitimacy?'

'I don't think people are too concerned about that nowadays.'

'Don't you! He gave a bark of bitter laughter. 'And how is Heather intending to support the two of them?'

'She's returning to work as soon as possible after the baby is born. Her mother will look after it,' Zee explained, wondering why he was so concerned when he hardly knew Heather.

'Every child should have its mother at home caring for it, especially during the early years.' Lorn stopped to lift the pushchair over a stony tract of shore, then set it down and confronted her. 'Don't you agree?'

'Yes, that's the ideal arrangement,' she admitted, 'but in some cases it's not possible and you have to make the best of the situation. Heather's child will be loved, surely that's the most important factor?'

'Yes.' It was an unwilling agreement.

'In any case, the child is her responsibility,' Zee ended up. 'You have no right to criticise.'

He raked a hand through his pale hair, tugging it from his brow. 'That's true.' He was abruptly contrite, his anger dissipated. 'But I can't help feeling sorry for the kid. It's starting out on life with the odds stacked against it.' He reached out a hand and stroked Emma's baby-soft cheek. 'Think how fortunate this little mite is by comparison. She has a proper birthright, a mother *and* a father.' He jerked up his eyebrows in sudden consternation. 'Or so I presume?'

Zee laughed, relieved that his fúry was spent. 'She has. Struan is her devoted daddy.'

'The guy who collected you last night?'

She nodded. 'He's my brother-in-law.'

They had reached the road. Lorn held the pushchair firm while Zee strapped in Emma. Sucking away at her thumb she was almost asleep, eyelids drooping.

'I thought perhaps he was your boy-friend,' he said, watching her.

Zee straightened up. 'I'm off men,' she glinted.

The corner of her mouth twitched. 'Not for life, I hope?'

'I doubt it, they do have some uses.'

'Sexual ones.'

The casual provocative comment sent her pulses skidding. He laughed at her startled expression, the dimple appearing and beguiling her. Briskly Zee strode forward, hands curled around the bar of the pushchair, head bowed to hide her eyes. When he had said that she had wanted to feel his arms around her—suddenly, strongly. She had been swamped by pure primitive desire. In bewilderment she shook the emotion away. She had wondered if she would ever feel desire again, after Mike. Now she had. And why should this particular man provoke such instant sexual emotion? Her chief reaction to him had been one of mistrust, so why this yearning? It was a purely instinctive animal thing, she decided, and was of no consequence. Veering, she puzzled over the true reason for his presence at Greenan Towers.

His mind was channelled towards the hotel, too. 'How do you come to be working at such a second-rate establishment?' he probed. 'Surely you're trained for something far better?'

Although grateful he had steered the conversation on to safer ground, his brutal assessment rankled, even if it was true. 'I have a degree in hotel management from Strathclyde University,' she said sharply. 'And Greenan Towers isn't so terrible.'

There was a grunt of scepticism in reply as he waited for more.

'I spent two and a half years at the Ecrepoint, but left at the end of the summer,' she continued.

'What line were you involved in?'

'When I left I was with the Public Relations Department, but it was part of a wider training scheme. I had worked in a variety of posts and was on the brink of becoming an Assistant Manager.' Her eyes shone. 'I hoped I would have gone even higher. It was a great experience. I loved working there.'

'Then why did you pack it in?'

His questions were beginning to feel like the Spanish Inquisition again and she was tempted to tell him to mind his own business. Instead she settled for a scathing look which was intended to put him in his place. It didn't. He smiled back with easy male confidence.

'A relationship with another member of the staff came to a rather fraught end,' she told him unwillingly. 'I felt it was impossible to continue working there.'

'Nonsense! Personal relationships shouldn't be allowed to interfere with your career.'

'I was rather impulsive,' she admitted, eyes downcast. 'I wish now I had had second thoughts. It was foolish to abandon a perfectly good job on Mike's account.'

'So you rushed out headlong and hurtled up to Scotland for a dose of home comfort?'

She shrugged. 'Perhaps, perhaps not. Though I must admit it's pleasant to be part of a family unit for a change. I'm staying with Carol and Struan, and their children. My parents are both dead.'

'How long do you intend to remain here?'

'Until Heather has had her baby and returned to work, then I shall hotfoot it down to London and find myself another job that's challenging, with prospects.'

'You really are a career woman!'

She disdained the taunting blue eyes. 'Definitely,' she confirmed.

'That man at the Ecrepoint must have been a louse,' he said, sharp eyes waiting for her reaction.

'Not particularly. He was your average Mister Nice Guy, expecting to be waited upon hand and foot.'

Lorn took a step back in mock horror. 'That's scathing!'

'But true,' she said bitterly.

'Why don't you apply for a transfer to one of the other Devenay hotels?' he suggested as they turned the corner of the road. 'They're not all like Greenan Towers. Some are first class, and have an excellent reputation. There's even one in Malaysia somewhere.'

'I didn't know that.'

'There is. Do you speak Malay?'

She nodded. 'A little, but I'm rusty now. There's not much call for it in Scotland.'

'I imagine not,' he chuckled. 'How long is it since you were in South-East Asia?'

'Five years. I haven't been back since my father died.' Her green eyes grew misty. 'It would be lovely to see all our old friends and servants again.' Briskly she shook away the fond memories. 'I'll certainly bear the Malay connection in mind, thanks for the information. You appear to be well informed about the Devenay company.'

'I told you, I read the business columns.'

Zee frowned. Something, somewhere didn't ring true. 'The Devenay chain would be a good bet for the future,' he continued. 'They're in the process of consolidating their position. Some of the hotels have already been streamlined and modernised where necessary.'

'Are consultants being used?' she asked. 'That's what happened at the Ecrepoint and turnover soared. They're well worth the money.'

Suddenly it hit her. She halted. Everything clicked into place. *That* was where she had seen him before, at the Ecrepoint just after she had started to work there. He was a director of the consultancy firm. She could vaguely remember him marching through the general office with the manager, and Mike, and an assortment of flunkeys in his wake. She spun to confront him. 'You underhand bastard! I know what you're doing at Greenan Towers. You're from that consultancy firm, J. and something.'

'J. & M. Consultancy Limited,' he supplied coolly.

'What a damn nerve!' Her face was pink with indignation. 'You arrive here pretending to be a regular guest, but all the time you've been checking up on us!'

'So?'

His calmness fuelled her anger. 'So it's a lousy trick, Mr Jensen, that's what!' Her knuckles whitened as she gripped the handle of the pushchair.

'It's standard practice,' he informed her diffidently. 'If managers are warned of my interest in advance they make sure the staff are on their best behaviour, which doesn't give a true reading of the situation. Managers are devious animals. They love to camouflage past failures. If my company is to be effective we need to know the full picture, warts and all.'

'You don't have a very high opinion of people's morals,' she flared.

'I'm a realist.' He put a large warm hand on top of hers and produced a coaxing smile. This time Zee was blind to the beguiling dimple, her eyes clouded with rage.

'Do you think you could keep quiet about my

identity for another day or so? I like to have all the facts at my fingertips before I reveal my true purpose.' He was deliberately turning on the charm. In other circumstances Zee would have been forced to admit it was considerable, but now his efforts were rejected. Incredulous with fury, she stared at him. He was asking her to betray her colleagues, to become his accomplice in his dirty deeds.

'Like hell!' she hurled, and left him.

CHAPTER THREE

ZEE's immediate instinct was to rush to the telephone and pass on the news of Lorn's real pupose at Greenan Towers to Mr McCrimmon. But she hesitated, mind whirling. In the past she had had cause to regret her 'on the spur of the moment' actions. Calm down, she told herself. Think carefully. Work out the implications. Once Lorn's identity was revealed he would snap into action, inspecting the accounts and poking his nose into every aspect of the day-to-day running of the hotel. Zee chewed frantically at her lip. Surely a wiser strategy would be to pretend to agree with his wish for anonymity? Then she could warn Mr McCrimmon in secret and allow him a breathing space in which to straighten out the worst of his blunders. Let's face it, if she was classified as a kitchen hand there must be other *faux pas* in the pipeline! She knew the manager was not criminally dishonest, it was merely that he was a bungler. At times he had bent the truth a little for the sake of a quiet life, and until now it *had* been quiet.

But no longer! Her heart missed a beat as she imagined the inevitable clash between Lorn and Mr McCrimmon. She didn't fancy the manager's chances at all. It had to be admitted that he was totally bereft of organisational skills, though always goodnatured. Lorn was a direct opposite. He would show no mercy. Even the smart professionalism of the Ecrepoint had been found wanting when it had fallen beneath his probing microscope, so what chance had Greenan Towers of meeting his demanding criteria? None. Lorn's approach was astute, implacable and as merciless as the guillotine. There was no hope.

With a sigh she considered the right way to break the news. It was imperative the subject be approached delicately. Mr McCrimmon could easily panic if she was too full of foreboding, and that would help no one. The right degree of caution must be found—somewhere between a casual comment and the four-minute warning! Zee spent the remainder of the afternoon composing a discreet alarm, but in the event it transpired her labours were for nothing, for when she returned to the hotel she discovered the manager was out for the evening.

'He's gone to see his friend, the accountant,' Aileen informed her.

So that was that, for the time being. She would have to wait until the morning to break the news. Lorn Jensen, too, had disappeared. There was no sign of the bronze Porsche, and Zee breathed a sigh of relief when ten o'clock arrived and he was still absent. The crisis had been postponed. At least she hadn't been forced to pretend she was willing to co-operate. That, too, was another hurdle to be confronted in the morning.

But the minute she stepped through the revolving doors at five to nine the next day, she realised all hell had been let loose. The atmosphere crackled with tension, and even before she had taken off her coat Heather was beckoning.

'That Mr Jensen is a consultant,' she hissed behind her hand, casting a sidelong glance at two guests who were settling their bills. Her voice dropped further. 'He's come to inspect Greenan Towers. The cheek of the man! Fancy him pretending to be a proper guest while all the time he was spying!'

Zee tried to look suitably surprised. While Heather was occupied she walked through to the cloakroom and hung up her coat. Taking a deep breath, she decided it promised to be quite a morning. With deft fingers she re-tied the brown and oyster-patterned silk scarf at her throat. The colours exactly matched her oyster-shaded wool jersey dress with its brown scalloping on collar and cuffs.

The two guests had departed when she returned to the reception counter, and it was only minutes before Aileen scurried out from the kitchen to join in Heather's vitriolic character assassination.

'I knew there was something odd about that Mr Jensen,' she declared in sharp tones. 'I never did trust him!'

'Where is he now?' Zee asked as Aileen glanced a third time towards the revolving doors.

'Out, and good riddance,' said Heather. 'Apparently he bowled in on poor Mr McCrimmon at the crack of dawn and told him why he was here. There's a formal meeting between the two of them fixed later this morning. For the past hour they've been measuring up the bedrooms and the lounge, and various other places. Then five minutes ago Mr Jensen shot off into town.'

'I hope he never comes back,' Aileen mumbled darkly.

'He will,' Heather predicted. 'He will.'

'Zee, can you bring your book, please?' Mr McCrimmon was calling from the doorway of his office.

With a nod she collected her pad and pencil.

'Poor wee thing,' Heather sighed as he disappeared again. 'He must be in a terrible state.'

He was. 'Oh dear, oh dear,' he moaned as Zee sat down before his desk. 'Have the girls told you what's happened?' He was wringing his hands, eyes darting back and forth across the pile of papers strewn over his desk. The room looked as though a bomb had hit it. Files were piled willy-nilly in a corner, drawers had been left half open, old accounts book lay on the floor.

'Perhaps it won't be as bad as you fear,' she said comfortingly, perfectly aware it would be ten times worse. 'Mr Jensen is here to help.'

'Help!' It was a cry of terror. Mr McCrimmon's eyes started out from his head as though he was about to suffer a fit. 'He's here to criticise, and he's already started. First thing this morning he demanded to know why the information Mr Edgar required wasn't available. Then when I couldn't produce a plan of the building and dimensions of all the rooms, he more or less accused me of malpractice.' He cracked his fingers in agitation. 'I've been up and down ladders for the past hour helping him take measurements. 'He's gone into Ayr now to see some architects.'

'Surely it can't be a bad thing if he spruces up the hotel?' she said by way of encouragement, but Mr McCrimmon wasn't listening.

'I don't like change,' he was muttering. 'Life has been running so smoothly, and now this cocky London upstart arrives and causes chaos!' He paused as a fresh thought struck him. 'No wonder Mr Edgar asked me to tighten things up. It was a warning there was an intruder in the camp. Still never mind, if the worst comes to the worst Mr Edgar will protect us from this—this. . . .' He ran out of suitable words.

'But Mr Edgar must have brought in the consultancy firm himself,' she pointed out in fairness.

His expression indicated that, whatever the real facts, he refused to believe the Chairman could have been so two-faced. Irrefutably the entire blame for the disruption of his world lay on the broad shoulders of the 'London upstart'.

'Mr Jensen'll be back around eleven,' he mumbled. 'He wants to check the accounts. Oh, and after lunch he intends to speak to the staff. Will you ask everyone to be in my office at two-thirty?'

Zee made a note on her pad.

'He was enquiring about fire insurance cover,' Mr McCrimmon continued, 'but I can't find records of the renewal payments. We'd better write to the company and ask for an up-to-date statement.'

Half an hour later Zee had taken down several similar letters, chasing matters which required clarification. Mr McCrimmon was clearly floundering, but how could she help? The filing system was a waste of time, though the relevant papers must be there somewhere. It

was impossible to know where to start. The files went
back to the year dot, and as Mr McCrimmon had
always done his own filing they were in a complete
muddle.

After she had typed the letters she collected an armful
of folders from the office and took them out to her
desk, where she began carefully working her way
through, rearranging everything into date order. It was
amazing what she found. A long-lost plumber's account
was discovered in the 'linen' file, and she unearthed a
tattered list of homegrown vegetables, proving that in
the dim and distant past old Jimmy *had* been effective
in the garden.

At a quarter to eleven, as she and Heather were
grabbing a quick coffee, Lorn came in.

'I trust I'm not interrupting anything important,' he
said, with a sarcastic glance at the cups on the desk.

Zee took a deep breath to control her temper.
'You're not, Mr Jensen,' she flashed back, but already
he had turned and was striding down the hall towards
the office, the sound of his feet on the parquet floor was
ominous as the tread of the Gestapo. An hour later Mr
McCrimmon called her in. To her surprise the desk top
had been cleared and Lorn sat in the winged chair
behind it, leaving the manager to perch anxiously on a
seat by his side. Lorn's impeachable air of authority
confirmed all her fears. He had taken full control.

He lost no time in coming to the point. 'Greenan
Towers is to be refurbished,' he told her briskly as she
sat down opposite him. 'Personally I consider the entire
operation to be a waste of time. The Devenay chain
would receive a far greater return if the hotel was sold
and the proceeds invested.'

From the edge of her vision Zee saw Mr McCrimmon
blanch.

'However, the Chairman is allowing his heart to rule
his head for the time being,' Lorn continued, with a wry
twist of his mouth. 'We have agreed I shall improve the
facilities, but work within a limited budget.' He threw a

scolding glance at Mr McCrimmon. 'Thus you have a second chance, but when the hotel is modernised I shall expect attitudes to be improved, too. In addition to material alterations there must be a distinct improvement in service.'

'Yes, Mr Jensen,' the manager replied meekly.

Lorn switched his attention to Zee. 'I shall be driving to Glasgow to consult with several architects on the alterations I have in mind. In the meantime I need names of local plumbers, electricians and painters. Firms with a good reputation.' He gave her a probing glance. 'I don't want a list copied from the Yellow Pages. I haven't time to waste, separating the wheat from the chaff—I expect you to do that for me. I need a short list of firms which deliver effectively, efficiently and on time. Understand?'

'Yes, sir,' she threw back, unable to keep the sharpness from her voice. He was barking out orders as though he was a sergeant-major and it was an effort to check her temper. For two pins she'd. . . .

'If you don't know which firms are good, give them a call,' he rapped. 'Pretend you have some job to be done and sound out reactions. Delete those who provide woolly answers. Time costs money, and *my* time comes expensive. I don't intend to become embroiled with halfwits who imagine tomorrow is soon enough.'

Lorn steamrollered on. As far as Zee could remember his approach hadn't fazed the Ecrepoint personnel. Despite a few grumbles, Mike had been full of admiration for J. & M. Consultancy Limited, but Mr McCrimmon was not so resilient. He was cowering beneath the flow of instructions. More directives, one following upon the other, were issued as Lorn worked his way down a near handwritten list. Now she knew why he had been so weary. He must have regularly worked into the early hours to amass such a plethora of information. She cast a worried glance at Mr McCrimmon. He seemed dazed. It was doubtful he was absorbing any of Lorn's commands. When Zee gave a small cough, Lorn looked up, hesitating in full spate.

'You'll discover the pace is slower here than in London,' she said tentatively, her heart in her mouth. She was outwardly calm, but inside she was quaking. It was a gamble, but if she could persuade him to cool down it would help matters.

'So I've noticed,' he rejoined, then following her eyes to the man beside him. The manager's dejection was plain to see. With obvious reluctance Lorn closed his notebook. 'Okay, that's enough for now. We'll take a half-hour break for lunch.'

'Half an hour?' Mr McCrimmon repeated in dismay.

'The quicker we work now, the sooner I'll be gone and leave you in peace.' Lorn was patronising.

At two-thirty the staff filed nervously into the office.

'Leave the door ajar, then you can keep an eye on the reception desk,' Lorn instructed Heather with a cynical lurch of his mouth. 'We can't afford to miss valuable customers.'

Zee glared at him, but he had bent his head and was inspecting papers on the desk. Chairs had been rustled up from the dining-room and everyone sat before him in two straight rows. Waiting like lambs to be slaughtered, she thought, casting a glance at old Jimmy. He had folded his arms grumpily and was watching Lorn with a suspicious eye. Jimmy hadn't wanted to come. None of them had, but if Lorn was aware of the tension in the air, he gave no indication.

'Good afternoon,' he said amicably, standing up and including every one in his smile. 'Thank you for sparing me your time.'

Sarcasm again, Zee decided, searching his face, but his expression was guileless.

'I'll explain what will be happening at Greenan Towers over the next few months,' he told his captive audience. 'My consultancy firm specialises in turning *un*profitable concerns into profitable ones, which is the reason the Devenay chain has retained us. Already we have worked on their hotels both in London and the States, and results so far are excellent. However,

Greenan Towers seems to be a special case.' He paused, straightening the pad on his desk as he allowed time for everyone to wonder at the significance of his words. 'Initially the bedrooms, lounge and dining-room will be modernised. Disruption will be kept to a minimum. The hotel may have to be closed for a period, probably in January, but all staff will be paid in full during that time. There don't appear to be many guests in winter, so there shouldn't be too much lost business. The central heating system and the kitchens will also be overhauled.' He directed his words to Mrs Weir. 'I must congratulate you on producing such fine food with such ramshackle equipment.'

For an instant his dimple appeared and Zee watched in disbelief and Mrs Weir blushed, coyly basking in the glow of the compliment. Indignation rose like bile in her throat. Minutes before entering the room the cook had been spouting full-blooded disapproval of Lorn, but now he appeared to have disarmed her with a single smile! Turning his attention back to the rest of the group, he continued. 'I shall be staying here for the next two weeks until the alterations are initiated. After that one of my executives will take my place, though I shall be travelling up to Scotland from time to time to check on progress.'

And woe betide anyone who's fallen behind, Zee thought peevishly.

'Also a staff training scheme will be organised—Miss Robertson could help there.' He flicked her a cool blue glance. 'And later someone will be transferred from another Devenay hotel to give a hand.' Putting both palms flat on the desk, he leant forward. 'Any questions?'

Mr McCrimmon cleared his throat. 'Do you—er—anticipate changes—er—in staffing?'

Reflectively Lorn pushed out his lower lip. 'At present—no.'

'But we'll take on extra folk when we're in the—er—five-star league?' Mr McCrimmon asked, beaming round, seeking approval at his attempted joke. Everyone laughed, grateful for release from the highly-charged atmosphere.

Patiently Lorn waited until they were all relaxed and then he sprang. 'You need extra guests, not extra staff,' he rasped. 'If they don't appear Greenan Towers will be shut down within the year.'

A startled gasp ricocheted around the room.

'Staff here needs to be upgraded, hence the training scheme,' he continued bluntly. For a moment he looked as though he was about to deliver an exasperated lecture, but then he thought better of it. 'Are there any suggestions on how to improve the image?'

Silence. Everyone sat mute, half through shock at his sudden revelation that their livelihood was in jeopardy, half through fear. His innate authority, heightened by his formal business approach and no-nonsense manner had mesmerised them all.

'If no one has anything to offer, we'll finish.'

It was dismissal. He had no further use for them. Silently the staff began to file from the room.

'Stay behind, please, Miss Robertson,' Lorn instructed, sitting down in the wing chair. 'And you, too, Mr McCrimmon.'

When the room was cleared he flipped open his cigarette case and offered it around. 'I've been checking the staff list,' he said, when he had lit cigarettes for himself and the manager. 'There's no mention of two receptionists, but I notice Miss Robertson appears as a kitchen hand.' He glanced at Zee and to her surprise she detected amusement hidden in the blue eyes. He took a long pull at his cigarette. 'I haven't noticed her doing much in the way of peeling potatoes.'

'Er—well—er. . . .' Desperately Mr McCrimmon started to explain.

Lorn stopped him. 'Don't worry.' He tapped a long finger on the list. 'I'm sure she's worth her salary, even if she is here under false pretences.' His face became serious again as he looked at her.

'Have you found names of suitable tradesmen?'

Producing a typed sheet, Zee handed it to him. Lorn studied it briefly, then scratched the back of his head. 'I'd like to visit these firms tomorrow morning to discuss my requirements. The trouble is I haven't been to Ayr before.' He turned to Mr McCrimmon. 'Would you allow Miss Robertson to act as my navigator?'

She knew he was merely going through the motions of civility. If he had asked Mr McCrimmon for permission for her to accompany him to the planet Venus approval would have been granted. There was no way the manager could refuse.

'Certainly, Mr Jensen,' came the expected reply.

'And I would be grateful if you would try to complete the financial statement.'

Zee felt he had unfairly stressed *try*, but while she began to fume with indignation, Mr McCrimmon only smiled. It was becoming apparent that from now on his policy would be to keep Lorn sweet, if that was remotely possible. She doubted it. After rattling off a few more instructions disguised as requests, Lorn swivelled his chair back to face her.

'Please make appointments for me at all those companies,' he indicated the list, 'and would you do some letters for me?'

Her brief nod of agreement was superfluous. He had taken it entirely for granted that she would work for him, which, on a reasonable basis, she supposed he was entitled to. But she didn't feel reasonable! She resented his interference and she resented the way the rest of the staff were already kow-towing. With an obsequious murmur Mr McCrimmon departed, offering Lorn full use of the office and telephone while he found a corner for himself at the reception desk. His subservience was infuriating. Why couldn't Lorn struggle through with makeshift accommodation? But that wasn't his style, as she was beginning to realise.

'Let's begin.' His tone was businesslike.

Her heart quailed when she saw the thick wad of

papers he had selected from his briefcase. The rate he set demanded full concentration. At best her shorthand was sketchy, and after weeks of Mr McCrimmon's stops and starts she was out of practice. She struggled to keep up with the dictation, determined not to lose face by asking Lorn to repeat himself. Mentally crossing her fingers, she trusted to luck that the hasty squiggles would make sense in translation. Adrenalin was bursting in her veins, flowing as it had never flowed since her arrival in Scotland. After forty minutes Lorn finished and she returned to her desk. Despite a smouldering resentment, she had to admit the work was a challenge. She had not felt stretched for months and after one or two heart-stopping moments when her shorthand seemed to be written in a foreign language, she began to enjoy herself. Brimming with satisfaction, she transcribed her notes and slipped the neatly typed letters into a folder. Lorn had removed his jacket and was working with shirtsleeves rolled up when she returned to the office. A haze of thick blue smoke hung on the air.

'You smoke too much,' she complained, wafting ineffectually at the pall. Zee placed the folder on his des. *His* desk. It hadn't taken him long. In one day he had effectively superseded Mr McCrimmon, making a lifetime's service count for nothing.

Ruefully he viewed the overflowing ashtray. 'It helps me relax.'

If this was Lorn relaxed, it was frightening to imagine what he would be like in top gear!

'You sound like Miss Canning,' he continued. 'She's always complaining, too.'

'Miss Canning?'

'My secretary. She usually travels with me on the various projects I'm involved with.'

Zee wondered what Miss Canning was like. Doubtless she was a leggy blonde, sophisticated and efficient, and as hard as nails, like her boss.

'Where is she now?' she asked.

'Her mother is ill, so she can't travel for the time being. I'm afraid I shall expect you to bear the brunt of the secretarial side of things for the next couple of weeks. Okay?'

It was obvious he expected her to jump to his aid without hesitation, but if she did, wasn't she going over to the enemy? When all was said and done, Mr McCrimmon and the staff desperately needed a champion. Divide and rule—that must be Lorn's plan. He required her allegiance. Folding her arms, she gave him a long level look.

'I really have no idea, sir. I suggest you ask Mr McCrimmon. After all, I do work for *him*.'

The fair head jerked up dangerously, his gaze hardening. 'Cut out the claptrap,' he ordered. 'Be realistic. You know as well as I do that Mr McCrimmon wields no power. I want you to work for me, so you will.' It was a command.

Her cat-green eyes flashed with anger. Hardly daring to breath she stared him out rebelliously. Who would weaken? Her expression tightened as she remembered playing a game at school, whoever blinked first was the loser. Time was suspended as emerald eyes clashed with ice blue. In the end Zee gave way. Whatever she did, he was bound to win. His authority was invincible. Taking a step forward, she gestured towards the folder. 'Can you sign the mail now, please. Then it will catch the early evening collection.'

Lorn was in the middle of reading the first sheet when abruptly he raised his head. 'I'm sorry, you shouldn't be working now,' he said, though his tone was impatient rather than apologetic. 'I'd forgotten you work in the evenings. Why didn't you remind me you had the afternoons free?' He glanced at his watch. 'Look, I'll drive you to the postbox and then home.'

She shook her head. 'I've only been helping out for the past two evenings because Agnes was unavailable, but her son's well again. I'm back on nine to five.'

'So you're free this evening?'

'Yes.'

'Which hotel has the best reputation for food around here?' he asked, scanning the letters.

'Craigdoon Country Club.'

'Right, we'll go there,' he said decisively. 'What time suits you? Around eight? Book us a table.'

'*We'll* go there?' she queried, watching him read and sign, read and sign. The sheer arrogance of the man took her breath away.

'You said you were free,' he reminded her, without looking up.

'Yes, but. . . .'

'I'll collect you just before eight.' With a flourish he sighed the final letter. 'Might as well inspect the opposition.' Pushing the papers back into the folder, he handed it to her. The smile and the groove in his cheek appeared. 'Thanks, you've worked well.'

Rising to his feet, Lorn slid open the top drawer of the filing cabinet. He frowned at the jumbled contents. 'We must go through this conglomeration together. Perhaps an evening would be the best time, no interruptions then.'

As if to prove his point, the telephone rang. He lifted the receiver. 'Hello, Clive, how's tricks?' he smiled, as the caller revealed his identity. With the diversion Zee was half forgotten. He put his hand over the mouthpiece for a moment. 'I thought you wanted to catch the post?' he said impatiently as she hesitated.

'I do,' she assured him, and hurried from the room.

'So you have a date with Mr Jensen! I thought you said he was unbearable,' Carol chuckled, eyes dancing.

'He is,' muttered Zee, squeezing cleansing lotion on to a cottonwool ball as she prepared to remove her make-up. 'I didn't have any choice. He railroaded me.'

'A likely story!'

'It's true. You should see him in action—he's unstoppable. He snaps out his orders and everyone rushes to do his bidding,' she declared peering at her reflection in the bathroom mirror.

'Including you? I thought you always kept men in their place?' Carol peaked an amused brow. 'Poor Mike didn't stand a chance.'

'In no way at all does Lorn resemble Mike,' Zee said heavily.

'Lorn is it now?' Her sister pounced on the unguarded familiarity as though it was a gift from heaven. 'Lorn Jensen.' She rolled the name around her mouth, tasting it. 'Sounds Scandinavian.'

Zee gave a sigh of exasperation. 'His father was Scottish and his mother is Danish.'

'Can't be,' Carol announced, watching as Zee wiped her face clean. 'If his name is Jensen it'll be his father who was Danish.'

She half shrugged. 'I must have it the wrong way round.'

'Ask him in for a sherry when he collects you,' her sister suggested. 'Then I can check him out.'

Arms akimbo, Zee spun round. 'No way! I'm not having you and Struan sizing him up as a prospective suitor. Heavens, you're far worse than any doting parents!' She bent to turn on the bath taps. 'The only reason we're dining together is to give him chance to see the Craigdoon Country Club. It's business, Carol.'

Her sister only chuckled again.

'An excellent meal,' Lorn leant back in his chair with a satisfied grin. 'Pleasant atmosphere, too.'

Zee sipped her coffee. The low-ceilinged dining-room with its rough grey stone walls, thick red carpet and flickering candlelight was appealing. A log fire crackled in an inglenook grate and unobtrusive waiters kept a watchful eye, refilling glasses and offering luscious desserts. Service had been quick and low key.

'Mrs Weir could do as well, given encouragement and extra help,' she insisted, setting down her cup.

'Loyal Miss Robertson,' he teased, arching a blond brow. 'Always first to the defence!'

Zee flushed. 'It's true,' she said indignantly.

'Yes,' he agreed mildly. 'Mind if I smoke?'

When she shook her head he lit a cigar, its aromatic fragrance drifting to her nostrils.

'Why have bar lunches never been provided at Greenan Towers?' he asked. 'They must be popular, virtually every other hotel in Ayr advertises them.' When he saw the look in her eyes he laughed. 'And if you dare to say "I really have no idea, sir" I shall come round to your side of the table and slowly strangle you!' His gaze raked over her flawless complexion and flaming hair. Her cinnamon-coloured dress was off-the-shoulder, gipsy style, exposing silken skin and a hint of soft full curves.

'Which would be a great shame,' Lorn continued, drinking in her beauty and the tantalising tilt of her breasts. 'Firstly because you're a delicious creature, and secondly because we've been getting along nicely together.'

The laughter in his eyes proved irresistible. Zee was forced to abandon her pique and return his smile. What he said was true. Her initial fears that the evening would consist of one lengthy complaint about the state of Greenan Towers had proved unfounded. Lorn had displayed an appealing sense of humour, and she had quickly felt at her ease. Indeed, the topic of the hotel had not been mentioned until she had leapt in with her comment about Mrs Weir. Time had flown as they discussed books and films, and faraway places.

'I love America!' Zee had said on discovering he had spent the bulk of the past year supervising alterations at Devenay States-side hotels. His periods in California explained the lingering golden tan.

'It's a great country,' he had agreed.

'Do you travel all the time?'

Lorn had brushed his moustache with the back of his hand. 'Roughly seventy per cent of my working life is spent abroad. I own a small mews cottage in central London, but I'm rarely there. Clive Masters, my partner, handles the majority of the U.K. business. He's married, with children, so the arrangement suits both of us. I'm free, he's not.' He shrugged. 'Naturally if I had family commitments we'd apportion the workload differently.'

Fleetingly her mind had drifted to his broken engagement, but then he had asked her about her years in Malaysia and she had been distracted.

'Bar lunches would go down well,' she agreed, coming back to the present. 'I dare say Mrs Weir could be persuaded to prepare them. She always growls at Mr McCrimmon if he suggests anything new and he backs down, but possibly you could be more successful.'

'I have more charm?' he asked, blue eyes crinkling at the corners with amusement.

Zee's thoughts flashed to his interplay with Mrs Weir at the meeting. So the charismatic approach had been deliberate! 'You ride roughshod over everyone,' she retorted.

He reached across the table and ran a cool fingertip across the back of her hand. Zee's pulses leapt to red alert at the light pressure.

'I didn't get where I am today by being negative,' he told her firmly. 'I know you consider me too harsh, but it's the way I play the game. Results speak for themselves. Clive and I formed the company five years ago and it's gone from strength to strength. Every concern we've handled, be it hotels, convention centres or supermarket chains, has shown a marked improvement in profit. Isolated units may have had to be sacrificed from time to time, but everyone has benefited in the long run.'

'I'm sure you're successful.' Her reply was tinged with a degree of reluctance which made him try harder.

'Look, Zee, if Greenan Towers had been left alone, sooner or later, and probably sooner, it would have gone to the wall. It's inevitable. It would have been closed down and everyone would have lost their jobs. Doing things my way you're all being given a second chance.' He had grabbed her hand and was holding it tightly, as if to emphasise the truth of his words.

'I suppose so.'

'For God's sake, throw away the emotional blinkers,' he ordered, his patience snapping. 'Use your common sense. Don't fight me, help me!' Irritation flickered in the intensity of his gaze. 'We could make a good team, but if you insist on siding against me, then just forget it.' He snatched his hand from hers and sat back, glowering. 'You can work with Mrs Weir in the kitchens where you're damn well supposed to be. I'll hire someone from an agency to cope with the secretarial side.

The impatient reaction unnerved her, but as he took an angry gulp of coffee her temper began to assert itself. 'So it's all or not at all?' she flared.

Without warning, Lorn smiled, the groove deepening in his cheek, leaving Zee with the curious sensation of having been dropped from a great height on to a feather bed.

'I want us to co-operate,' he said gently, reaching across and recapturing her fingers. 'I'm sorry if you think I'm pushing. Perhaps I do come on too strong at times, but I'm not willing to settle for second best. Either you work for me, with me, wholeheartedly, or we make other arrangements.' His mouth twisted pleadingly. 'It'll be better for both of us if we trust each other.'

'Yes,' she agreed, gathering her wits. Most of his message had been harsh, but the caress of his fingers and the seductive warmth which now shone from his eyes were disarming her.

'You're an intelligent woman,' he said. 'What improvements would you make at Greenan Towers?'

The same question had come from Mr McCrimmon, but this time Zee knew that if Lorn was in agreement her suggestions would be implemented at high speed. After a pause she succumbed to his waiting interest.

'I would accentuate the Scottish angle, include haggis

and neeps, clooty dumplings and such like, on the menu.'

'With subtitles provided for the Sassenachs,' he grinned. 'Neeps means turnips. Clooty dumplings are fruit puddings.'

She nodded. 'In the summer I'd organise Highland dancing on the back lawn—there are several schools in town which could supply dancers. And I might have a piper, or even coax old Jimmy into a kilt.'

'He needs to be retired,' Lorn cut in sharply.

Zee ignored him. 'I'd dress the waistresses in tartan, and present lady guests with a sprig of white heather.' Her enthusiasm was carrying her forward. 'I'd show films about Scotland on rainy days and advertise like mad in the States. Americans are fascinated with history, and many of them have Scottish ancestry. Motor coaches could be arranged to take them round the old castles and churches, or they could follow the Burns' Heritage Trail, visiting the places connected with Robbie Burns.' She took a breath. 'And they could drive along the Electric Brae.'

'What's that?' he interrupted.

'It's a hill on the southern coast road. When you think you're travelling downhill, you're actually going uphill, and vice versa.'

'Sounds intriguing,' he grinned. 'You must take me there.'

His dimple was bewitching her. Zee decided to risk all. 'And if I were *you*, Mr Lorn Jensen,' she continued, her expression tightening, 'I'd do my best to improve my public relations image.'

He stiffened, raising his chin a fraction, and taking a long guarded drag on his cigar. 'And what does that mean?' he asked, a thread of menace in his tone.

Her heart quickened its beat. He was taking stock of her, eyes narrowed, muscles tense. Zee knew that if she put a foot wrong, he would attack without mercy. Taking a deep breath, she ploughed on. 'Your incisive attitude might be accepted in more sophisticated areas where people are in tune with rapid decision making, but I suggest you tone it down here. There'll be less friction if you wear a velvet glove over that iron hand.'

The corner of his mouth crooked as he glanced down at his fist.

'Aileen is terrified of you, and Heather is hardly a cheer-leader for your team either,' she continued. 'Likewise Mr McCrimmon and the rest of the staff, but if you slacken off half a notch, coax instead of issuing ultimatums, life will be easier.' There was a pregnant pause. '*Easier*,' she stressed, 'not slacker.'

Slowly Lorn exhaled a cloud of cigar smoke. 'I'll try, Zee,' he promised with uncharacteristic meekness, and smiled at her surprise.

It was after eleven when he drove her back to Carol's house. As he pulled the Porsche to a halt outside the front gate, a curtain in the lounge window twitched and fell still.

'Thanks for the evening, I've enjoyed myself,' she smiled. Surprisingly enough, she had. Despite a few reservations she was on his side, though she didn't quite know how she came to be there. He had made sense when he said they should co-operate, and Lorn seemed satisfied that they were now in double harness. Yet she hadn't teamed up of her own volition. He was devious as well as forceful, she realised.

'Goodnight.' Zee reached for the door handle, but before she could move he leaned forward and brushed his lips across her brow. The stiff hairs of his moustache made her skin tingle and she moved her head a fraction, enjoying the sensation. It was a new and different feeling.

'You like moustaches?' he asked. The car was dark, his face in shadow.

'I've never been out with a man with a moustache before,' she confessed.

'Then it's time to experiment,' he said, the smile coming through.

Before she could protest he had slipped an arm around her shoulders and was pulling her close. His mouth claimed hers. The firm touch of his lips and the roughness of his moustache was a heady combination. Without warning the desire she had experienced on the beach took over and unthinkingly she slid an arm around his neck. As he coaxed her lips apart she sighed, surrendering to the virile masculinity of his touch and taste. Oblivious to reason, she accepted his caress then, as his kiss deepened, she remembered who he was. Not exactly the enemy any more, but certainly not a friend. Extricating herself from his grasp, she fumbled for the door handle.

'How was that?' he asked.

She could see the gleam of his smile in the dark. His smug delight caught hold of her breath and tossed it away. He knew damn well she had enjoyed their contact! Stepping out on to the pavement, she swivelled to face him.

'Not bad,' she announced crisply. 'I now know what it's like to kiss a porcupine.'

'Whatever turns you on,' he shot back, but he was laughing as he drove away.

'Take it or leave it,' Lorn pronounced, lolling back in his chair. 'If you want the business then you must be prepared to work the hours specified, within the stipulated time limit, not forgetting the penalty clause, and you must use the itemised products.' There was a flicker of a smile. 'In return you have a good day's pay for a good day's work.'

From her seat at the other desk, Zee waited for the reply.

'Take it or leave it,' was Lorn's chant. This tradesman was only one of several to be speared with the ultimatum, for despite Lorn's promise to soft-pedal, there had been little sign of flexibility in his business methods. Reflectively she nibbled at the tip of a thumbnail. After days of dealings with plumbers and electricians and the like, she was reluctantly coming round to Lorn's point of view. Never had she heard so many vague promises, ducked decisions and halfhearted agreements. But fortunately among the floss were firms prepared to work well and keep to their word. Lorn had ruthlessly selected the cream.

The man before him inspected his notebook again. 'You require a firm commitment, Mr Jensen?'

The fair head nodded. 'I do.'

'Then yes, sir, we'll start next week. There are one or two other jobs booked, but we'll push those aside and do your work first.'

Lorn leapt to his feet, hand outstretched, a gleam of triumph in his eyes. 'Thank you,' he said, shaking hands as he steered the man out of the room.

Zee scribbled a note on her pad. Now there was one outstanding job to be finalised. Lorn certainly functioned on high-octane fuel, for over the past ten days he had worked non-stop. They both had. After the first morning when he had worn a path, stomping between the office and her desk in reception, he had lost patience. Now she was based in his office, where he used her as a sounding board, a secretary, a team-mate. She had never felt so vibrantly alive, for working with Lorn was downright exhilarating. Again she checked her notes. Two telephone calls were scheduled with the States, and Mr Edgar had asked if Lorn would ring him when he was free. Consulting her watch she rose and walked towards the door, but abruptly it was flung open as Lorn strode in.

'I wanted him and I got him,' he cheered smugly.

'You have to phone Mr Edgar,' she began, but her voice faded.

Kicking backwards with his foot, Lorn had slammed shut the door and taken a step towards her, his face suddenly solemn. His penetrating blue eyes sought and held hers. The mood had changed, making Zee's heart slip and slide, while every fibre of her body shouted caution. The atmosphere was rich with the throb of electricity.

For ten days they had worked together. Until late in the evening they had tried to make sense of the files, and on other occasions he had taken her out to dinner. 'To test the opposition,' he had said, but Zee was becoming increasingly aware of a sexual undercurrent which was growing stronger with each contact. Desire for him had flared, but so far she had controlled it, staying deliberately cool in his arms when he had kissed her. Feminine instinct warned her Lorn was capable of making her lose her head, and she had no intention of allowing that to happen. Her experience with Mike had made her wary, and it seemed only wise to keep her friendship with Lorn on a low key.

He took another step forward and slid both hands around her waist, his fingers firm. She could feel each one separately though her fine silk blouse. As he kissed her neck his breathing quickened, his heart bumping against hers. Shakily she smiled, spreading her hands against his chest.

'You must phone Mr Edgar,' she repeated, inspecting her watch. 'Before five, which only gives you a few minutes.'

The Chairman had not been specific on time, but Lorn would never know.

With a short sharp swear-word, he released her. The look in his eyes told her he had wanted, and expected, more than a brief hug. She had quickly realised Lorn was a passionate man, and would have no compunction about railroading her with the same lethal skill he showed on the tradesmen. If he realised the fragility of her defences, he would pounce. A shivering thrill ran down her spine. She was becoming addicted to Lorn, but he was a narcotic she could well do without. As he waited for Heather on the switchboard to obtain the number, he winked, making her heart lurch.

'I'll go and check tomorrow's order with Mrs Weir,' she said, preparing her escape.

He nodded, and when the call was connected unbuttoned his jacket and sprawled back in his chair, concentration creasing his brow.

'Lorn here, Edgar.'

The familiarity of his relationship with the Chairman had been a surprise. The normal business scenario was missing. Lorn treated Edgar with scant respect. He *told* him what was happening at Greenan Towers and as far as Zee knew Lorn's decisions were never questioned. She could only presume that as J. & M. Consultancy had proved so successful in the past, Lorn had been given *carte blanche* where future projects were concerned. Closing the door quietly behind her, she walked through to the kitchen.

Mrs Weir was peeling mushrooms. Zee lifted the lid of a large casserole where browned beef and onions lay waiting. 'What are you making?'

'Boeuf bourguignon.' The cook sliced briskly through the white stalks. 'Our Mr Jensen thought it would make a change.'

Zee smothered a smile. *Our* Mr Jensen, was it? Lorn had taken her advice when it came to dealing with the staff, his softer approach paying dividends. Mrs Weir had happily fallen in with his ideas and was already planning bar lunches for the spring, in addition to experimenting with fresh dishes on the dinner menu.

'He enjoyed the scampi in cheese sauce last night,' she continued, her plump face a trifle smug. 'Came through especially to tell me how good it was.' The mushrooms were sprinkled into the casserole dish. 'I thought I might try Baked Alaska this evening. I know he has a sweet tooth.'

Zee wrote down the grocery requirements which would be telephoned through to the warehouse first thing in the morning, listening all the time to Mrs Weir's glowing comments on *our* Mr Jensen. When she returned to the office Lorn had finished his call.

'You've certainly twisted Mrs Weir around your little finger,' she teased as she sat down.

'Thanks to you. You're a good influence on me. We work well together.' He stretched and rose to his feet, walking across the worn carpet to her desk. Without a word he took hold of both her hands and pulled her upright beside him. Her nerves began to leap erratically as he slid his hands beneath her suit jacket and up on to her shoulder blades, pressing her close so that her breasts were against his chest. His jacket was open, and the heat of him through the thin poplin burned into her, fusing them together. His hands moved compulsively lower to her waist, and then down to her hips, sculpting her to him.

'Zee, darling Zee,' he murmured, and her resistance began to waver.

The jagged shrill of the telephone startled them both. Zee recovered first. 'That'll be one of your American calls,' she said, pushing him in the direction of the telephone.

Lorn cursed softly. As he lifted the receiver he leant back on the edge of his desk, watching her in a steady measured way which made her pulses scamper.

'Yes, I'll hang on,' he said, pushing his free hand into his trouser pocket. He rested the mouthpiece against his shoulder. 'In a couple of weeks' time we're going away together, Zee,' he grinned. 'To Malaysia—the Devenay hotel in Kuala Kuning is next on my list.'

CHAPTER FOUR

ZEE's emerald eyes widened in surprise. 'But—but can't your secretary go?'

Shifting the receiver to his other hand, Lorn beckoned her. It never crossed her mind to disobey. When she joined him he slid an arm around the warm supple curve of her waist and began to nuzzle at her forehead, his moustache tantalising the tenderness of her skin.

'I want you,' he murmured, and the desire darkening his eyes told her exactly what he meant. He pulled her close, until she was resting against him with her full weight. Her temperature soared as his hand moved inside her jacket and travelled up across her ribcage to the side of her breast, stilling as his fingers explored the soft fullness and the hardening peak. Lorn's breathing became deeper, his desire stronger. He was bending his head to kiss her mouth, when there was a crackle on the telephone. For a moment he was confused, then he gave his head a little shake.

'Lorn—Lorn Jensen here,' he said, straightening up but keeping a firm hold of Zee. As he started to speak she slithered her hand across his shirt front and began to ease open a button. She wanted to stroke him, to love him. She knew she was acting impulsively again, but she no longer cared.

'God!' he muttered softly as her fingers caressed his skin. The muscles beneath her touch tightened. Reluctantly Lorn returned to the business discussion, his voice becoming hard and decisive. Zee was dimly aware of an argument about delivery of sprinklers and fire doors. There appeared to be some delay, but she was too happily engrossed to pay much attention. The feel of Lorn's hairy chest was lighting fires within her, creating an erotic need which she had not felt before, certainly never with Mike. Three buttons were freed. Spreading her hands, she slid them across his chest. He gave a silent gasp as her fingertips grazed his nipples, but continued snapping out directives. Zee kissed the firm golden skin, teasing it with the tip of her tongue.

'God!' he moaned, raising his head, then 'Okay, okay. If we have to wait, we have to wait!' he barked. He dropped the telephone back on to its rest and his arms tightened around her like bands of living steel. 'How the hell am I supposed to conduct a sensible conversation when you're touching me like that? he whispered, kissing her ear.

'I really have no idea, sir,' she teased, green eyes sparkling.

Lorn grinned. 'You deserve to be punished for that, my darling.' He gave a husky growl and nibbled at her neck. His breathing was ragged. He shifted his hip, dragging her hard against his thighs. 'You know, Zee, it should be me undressing you,' he complained, sliding his fingers to the neckline of her blouse.

The sound of footsteps in the hall made them jump guiltily apart. Zee scuttled back to her desk and had only just sat down as a knock came at the door. Mr McCrimmon appeared. Lorn turned away towards the filing cabinet, hurriedly fastening his shirt.

'Do you know where the fire insurance papers are kept, Miss Robertson?' he asked in a cool voice. When he swung round only the crooked line of his tie indicated their lovemaking of a moment ago.

'Second drawer,' she replied, her businesslike tone matching his.

He reached down. 'Can you spare Miss Robertson for two weeks at the beginning of December?' he asked, slapping a folder on to his desk. 'I need her to translate for me in Malaysia. My own secretary is unable to travel. We'll be back before Christmas,' he added, when there was no reply.

'But supposing Heather has her baby early?' Mr McCrimmon asked.

Lorn glared at him impatiently. 'Then you hire someone from an agency,' he snapped, railroading again.

'Typical impetuous Zee,' Carol sighed. 'Perfectly prepared to shoot off into the wide blue yonder with some man she hardly knows!' She arched a teasing brow.

'I *do* know him,' Zee protested.

Her sister hitched Gordie further on to her hip and gazed out at the bleak pale sky. 'I must confess I envy you. What I'd give for a spell in the tropics!'

'See what comes your way if you're single,' Zee grinned, stretching her palms to the glow of the coal fire. 'I shall spare you a thought shivering here, while I'm lying in my bikini beneath the blaze of the noonday sun.'

Carol swivelled. 'I thought this was a business trip! Though the idea of acting as a translator seems stupid to me. You know, most Malays speak some English and certainly those working in the hotel trade are fluent.'

'I've explained that,' she said airily, 'but Lorn needs secretarial help.'

'You're not even a proper secretary!'

'I know, and once I leave Greenan Towers I shall quickly revert to doing what I enjoy best—hotel management.' She shrugged. 'But this really is too good an opportunity to miss.'

'And you think you'll be able to visit Habsah? You lucky girl, I'll write and tell her you're coming.' Carol's face clouded. 'I still miss her, Zee. I wish she could see Emma and Gordie, she'd be so thrilled with them.' She smoothed down her son's silken head. 'I love her so much. She's much more like a proper mother than Mum ever was. I hope that next year she'll be able to come and visit us.'

Zee smiled tenderly; she loved Habsah too. Throughout their childhood their mother had been in poor health, and had died when Zee was twelve and Carol ten. Her memories were of a shadowy figure lying in bed, constantly bemoaning her lot. Habsah, their Malay *amah*, was a girl of twenty-four when Mrs Robertson had finally faded into the relief of death, and by that time she was running the household and filling the role of mother far more competently than the original incumbent. She also occupied the position of wife. Although her father and Habsah had acted discreetly, over the years Zee had accepted that the brown-skinned girl shared her father's bed. When he died he had left Habsah a generous legacy, and she had moved into her own bungalow near Port Dickson.

'The Devenay hotel is on the east coast, hundreds of miles cross-country from Habsah's home, but Lorn is happy for me to take a few days off at the end of our stay in order to visit her,' Zee explained.

'When do I have the chance to inspect this Lorn and check that he's trustworthy?' Carol grumbled, sitting Gordie down in the corner of the sofa. 'You're very secretive about him.'

'I'm not,' she protested, 'but I won't allow you to look him over as a future brother-in-law. He's very nice, but you know my views on marriage. I'm playing it cool, that's all.'

But not cool enough, she cautioned herself. Every morning she went into Greenan Towers determined to edge their relationship on to a more businesslike footing, but without success. There was a sensual filament of awareness which stretched between them, entwining them closer and closer. Ever since the episode in the office when she had rashly followed her emotions and unfastened Lorn's shirt, she had kept herself under strick control.

'This isn't the right place,' she had told him with false calm the following morning when he had put his arms around her and drawn her close. 'Someone will come in.'

For a long moment he had studied her, but Zee had returned his look with steadfast eyes.

'You're right,' he had agreed with a sigh. 'Not in working hours.' Burying himself in commercial matters, he had obeyed her wishes, and when he had asked her to dinner that evening she had made the excuse of babysitting for Carol, deliberately not suggesting he join her. Temptation would be too great if they were alone together. Frequently she had sensed his mind wandering, his eyes swivelling to her, and she had kept her head down, outwardly concentrating on the papers before her, while her mind jack-knifed alarmingly. Common sense decreed it was unwise to go with Lorn to Malaysia, and the urge to cancel the arrangement flowed and ebbed. Unhappily she knew that if she refused to go he was quite capable of shutting her out of his life for ever, and that made her hesitate. . . . But why? What did he want of her? And, more to the point, what did she want of him? Her feelings were illogical. She rebelled against his 'take it or leave it' attitude. Perhaps if they became further entangled he would claim more than she was prepared to give? And yet already she sensed that life without Lorn would be an anticlimax. What she desired was a cosy undemanding place in his affections. A small voice screamed that Lorn wasn't a cosy undemanding man. If he had been, she wouldn't have been interested in him in the first place.

'I'm returning to London tomorrow,' said Lorn as she entered the office the next morning. 'Everything is organised here, there's nothing more for me to do. I want you to keep everyone up to scratch, Zee.'

She quelled her fluttering dismay at the news of his departure. 'You mean bark at them?' she asked lightly.

He grinned. 'A flash of your long legs would be more effective.' Becoming serious, he took the gold case from his breast pocket and extracted a cigarette. 'I have to fly over to the States to sort out some problems there, but I'll be back in time for our visit to Malaysia. I'll meet you at Heathrow.' He snapped on his lighter and inhaled from the flame, the tip of his cigarette glowing red. 'When you leave Greenan Towers I shall send Miles Lang to take charge. He's one of my young executives.'

'Does he bark like you?' she glinted.

'No, and that's why he'll never run his own company, but he *is* efficient,' Lorn retorted, walking across to the window. He looked out at the winter sunshine. 'It's a nice day. Shall we have a drive around the district and you can show me all those tourist traps?'

'But I have letters to type,' she protested.

'Leave them. You can do them tomorrow and sign them on my behalf.'

Before she could think up any more reasons for not going, Lorn had ordered her out to collect her coat.

'Right, ma'am, I'm in your hands,' he grinned, swinging the low car out of the hotel forecourt on to the road. Beside him Zee was snug in her brown cape coat and high leather boots.

'Burns' Statue first,' she decreed, 'then his cottage, Alloway Kirk, the Monument and the Brig o'Doon.'

Lorn reached across and squeezed her knee. 'Sounds hectic.'

'A whistle-stop tour,' she agreed, removing his hand.

The morning sped by. Zee took great pleasure in showing off the heritage of her homeland, especially as Lorn was properly appreciative.

'All your hypothetical Americans are going to love this,' he declared as they strode up the cobbled slope of the Auld Brig o'Doon. They stood together on the peaked arch of the ancient stone bridge gazing down into the crystal-clear waters which flowed beneath. Smooth green lawns swept down to the river, and in the distance, bathed in the sharp winter sunshine, was the tall edifice of the Burns' Monument with its Corinthian pillars and ornamented cupola.

'This bridge is supposed to date back to the fifteenth century,' Zee recited. 'Tam o'Shanter escaped from the witches by running across it in Robbie Burns' poem.'

'The true tourist guide,' he teased, taking her hand.

She hardened herself against the warmth in his eyes, the thrilling rub of his thumb on her palm. 'Come on,' she said, more sharply than she had intended. 'Next stop is the Electric Brae.'

The azure blue of the sky was mirrored in the sea as they took the coast road and drove south. Smooth green hills rolled indolently inland while seawards the wide expanse of blue stretched to the horizon.

'Slow down,' Zee warned as the road curved around the crest of a headland. 'Now, are we travelling uphill or down?'

Lorn studied their surroundings. The grey tarmac road was ribbon narrow, hedges on either side, the fields beyond. A whitewashed cottage nestled in the valley below. 'I'm bound to be wrong,' he admitted ruefully, 'but I'd guess we're going downhill.'

'Switch off the engine and let the car roll.'

Checking that the road was clear, he did as he was told and raised astonished brows as the Porsche began to slide slowly backwards.

Zee laughed at his look of disbelief. 'It's an optical illusion, something to do with the contours of the land.'

They drove on along the coast to the little fishing port of Girvan where they had lunch and explored the harbour. When they returned in the late afternoon, Lorn insisted on stopping at the Electric Brae again. 'Incredible,' he said, shaking his fair head in amusement.

The sky was flushed with the pinks and blues of a setting sun when they arrive back at Carol's. Lorn pulled the car to a halt at the kerb. 'Have dinner with me—please,' he added softly. 'It's my last evening in Ayr. I shan't see you for nearly two weeks.'

'I can't. I'm babysitting.'

This time it was true. Carol and Struan had been

invited out to supper with friends. Lorn took hold of her chin in his hand, forcing her to face him. 'You're avoiding me, Zee,' he challenged. 'Why?'

Evasively she lowered thick dark lashes. 'I'm not.'

'Look at me,' he instructed, his fingers tightening.

Wide green eyes were lifted to meet his.

'You're driving me insane,' he muttered, and a nerve throbbed in his temple. He was bending his head to kiss her when there was a series of taps on the car window, and Zee twisted from him in surprise. Carol was stood on the pavement, smiling broadly, eyes devouring Lorn. She waited as she wound down the window.

'Hello. I wondered if you would both like to come in for a cup of coffee.'

Zee pressed her lips together in a tight line and glared—no, no, *no*! but her sister was immune.

'Sounds like a good idea,' Lorn smiled, unaware of the interchange.

'I've heard so much about you,' gushed Carol, leading the way to the front door.

Zee cringed. 'Just you wait!' she hissed as she swept past into the house, but her threat held no fears and Carol chatted gaily as she produced coffee and shortbread.

'Do you specialise in bringing hotels up to date?' she asked.

Lorn kept a watchful eye on the coffee cup balanced on the arm of his chair, as Emma deposited interlocking plastic bricks in his lap.

'Make a plane,' she commanded.

'Hotels are in my blood to a certain extent,' he smiled. 'I studied Business Management at university and later had a stint at Harvard. My partner, Clive Masters was there too. We each went on to work for different management consultants, but after a time decided to pool our resources.'

'Zee tells me you work very hard.'

'I do,' he agreed, splicing the plastic bricks together. 'I'm ambitious.'

'So's Zee,' Carol said smoothly. 'She maintains she's a hundred per cent career woman, all press-button efficiency and no heart. Can't you just imagine what she'll be like when she's thirty-five? Frigidly professional, with her own apartment, own car and two cats!'

'No, I can't imagine that,' said Lorn, grinning across at a glowering Zee.

'We don't all feel the urge to wallow in nappies and running noses,' she retorted, wishing she could annihilate her sister. 'In any case, I can always have a bash at domesticity when I'm older. Plenty of women do.'

'You'll be past it when you're thirty-five,' Carol taunted.

Lorn leapt gallantly to the rescue. 'Nonsense! She'll be very attractive. Good bone structure, long legs and that gorgeous red hair—she'll be a stunner!'

'Thank you,' she said smugly, resisting the temptation to poke her tongue out at Carol. Recklessly gratitude got the better of her and she found herself asking Lorn if he would join her for dinner while she was babysitting. 'It'll be pot luck,' she emphasised, already wondering what had prompted her rash action.

'That's fine,' he smiled. He handed an aeroplane of sorts to Emma. 'I'm afraid that's the best I can do.' He raised a laughing brow at the lopsided structure and rose to his feet. 'I'd better get back to Greenan Towers and check if there've been any phone calls which need my attention.'

'See you around eight,' said Zee as she waved goodbye.

The clock showed almost half-past when he arrived. She was grateful he had been delayed for Carol had hung around, itching to see him again.

'I'd grab him quick,' she said, as Struan led her out to the car.

After they had gone Zee straightened the cushions on the settee and tidied away stray toys. The table was already set, everything prepared, and soft music floated from the stereo. Her chic clothes had been discarded, and she was casual in tight denims and a blue and white checked shirt. Her thick hair, cut blunt, fell in a straight polished curtain to her shoulders, a geometrical parting dead centre. Two fine plaits swung at one side of her face, fastened with tiny blue beads.

'Sorry I'm late,' Lorn apologised, handing her a bottle of wine. 'There was another crisis in the States. I've been on the telephone non-stop since I left you.' Wearily he ran his fingers through his hair. 'Are the children in bed?' he asked, walking with her into the kitchen. As if on cue a wail came from upstairs.

'They are, but Gordie is teething,' Zee groaned. 'According to Carol he's been teething constantly since he was born.' She put her head on one side and listened, waiting. Lorn watched as the two slender plaits brushed her cheek. She looked softer, more vulnerable without the sophisticated veneer of her working clothes. Another cry came, then another and another, gathering momentum.

Zee pulled a face. 'I'd better go up and see what's the matter.'

'I'll come with you.'

Lorn followed her up the stairs. Light from the landing shone into the small bedroom, illuminating Gordie in his teddy-bear patterned pyjamas. He was holding on to the rails of his cot, plump tears spilling down his cheeks. Zee held him against her shoulder comforting him, and when she patted his back he hiccuped.

'Wind,' Lorn pronounced, with the ghost of a chuckle. In dark blue sweatshirt and matching cords he was resting a wide shoulder against the door frame, watching her. Zee laid the baby down and tucked him in. Tiptoeing from the room, she reached the landing and waited. Silence.

'I'll check on Emma, she always kicks off her covers,' she whispered.

Emma was spreadeagled on her stomach, sheets and blankets crumpled on the bedroom floor. Silently Zee pulled them back over he sleeping child and secured them, then crept out towards Lorn in the doorway. Not moving, he blocked her exit, and as she came near he reached out, encircling her in his arms. His mouth descended and Zee came halfway to meet it, knowing she was playing with fire, her own fire and Lorn's.

'I wish you'd tuck me up in bed and climb in beside me,' he murmured, confirming her thoughts. Emma stirred in her sleep and Lorn looked up, giving Zee the impetus needed to break away.

'Let's go downstairs and I'll make us a cheese omelette,' she said, escaping.

'I can't understand why you're so set against marriage when you're so fond of children,' Lorn remarked, lolling against the worktop in the kitchen.

'Let's just say I had my eyes opened.' Zee smartly cracked an egg against the rim of the mixing bowl.

'By the man at the Ecrepoint?'

'Yes.' She added more eggs and picked up the whisk. Her wrist moved rhythmically as she began to beat the mixture. 'I thought I was in love with Mike. I was sharing a flat with two girls and about the same time that one of them left, Mike's lease on his flat expired.' Zee sighed. 'I suggested he moved in with Tricia and me.'

Lorn was standing very still, hands in his trouser pockets, watching her. 'And what happened?'

The whisk's tempo accelerated. 'We—we weren't compatible. We'd agreed I had just as much right to a career as he did and that when we were married everything would be on an equal basis, but after six weeks I realised he'd only been paying lip service.' Her eyes were suspiciously bright. 'And—and there were other indications that we'd never make a go of it, so—so I moved out.'

'After only *six* weeks! You didn't give the guy much of a chance, did you? In any case, two of you sharing accommodation with a third person was no indication of what married life would be like.'

'Tricia had nothing to do with it,' Zee declared, pouring the egg mixture into a heated frying pan. She took a chunk of cheese from the fridge.

'It sounds to me as though you rushed blindly into the situation and then rushed blindly out again,' Lorn accused. 'You couldn't have loved him very much.'

Zee pivoted to glare at him. 'Okay, so I was impetuous, I admit that, but I did think I loved him. It hurt like hell when I left, but there was no alternative. All Mike wanted was someone to wash his shirts, cook his meals and look after him.'

'And that was a crime?' Lorn queried.

'It wasn't equality,' she mumbled.

'Equality doesn't mean splitting every task right down the middle. Isn't it a case of co-operation? One partner dealing with some chores while the other copes with different things.'

She sprinkled grated cheese and herbs on to the fluffy omelette and took warm plates from the oven. A crisp green salad was waiting on the table in the dining area.

'All Mike wanted to do was play rugby and make love.'

Lorn chuckled. 'Sounds a sensible kind of guy, though I'd scrap the rugby myself.'

Zee grinned, her mood lifting. 'You men are all the same!'

'We're not,' Lorn assured her, uncorking the wine. 'Oh no, we're not.'

The dry white wine went down well with the omelette and salad. Zee produced a fruit pavlova with fresh cream for dessert. They dawdled happily over coffee, discussing the historical places they had visited that morning.

'I'll help you with the dishes,' said Lorn, when they had drained the coffee pot.

'You're only on your best behaviour because of my

tirade against Mike,' she teased, stacking the dirty plates in the sink.

Lorn gave an elegant shrug as he picked up the tea towel. 'I *have* lived alone for several years, so I've grasped the mechanics of washing up.'

When she had finished, Zee dried her hands and watched as he put the last cup away in the cupboard. She found it surprising such a powerful male ego didn't baulk at domesticity, for Mike had invariably dredged up some excuse.

'You're very. . . .' There was a yell from upstairs and she stopped mid-sentence.

'More wind,' Lorn chuckled, as Zee cocked her head and waited. The yells increased in volume.

'Would you like to pour yourself a brandy while I attend to Carol's son and heir?' she suggested with a sigh.

This time it was something more than wind, for Gordie refused at first to be comforted. Zee patted his back, changed his nappy, cuddled him, but it was only when she finally dabbed teething gel on to his firey gums that he quietened. With a sigh of relief she laid him down in his cot and pulled up the covers. When she went downstairs the stereo was playing a plaintive love song and Lorn was lying full length on the settee, eyes closed. His shoes had been kicked off and the empty brandy goblet was on a side table. For a few moments she watched him in the muted light, enjoying the raw maleness of him. His blond hair was tousled across his brow. He had stuck his thumbs into his wide leather belt and his fingers were spread across the flat of his stomach. The muscles of his thighs were outlined by the tight corduroy trousers. Zee tried to ignore the fact that her heart was beating a little quicker as she walked forward.

Lazily Lorn came to life. 'Sorry,' he said, rubbing his eyes. 'I've been burning too much midnight oil and it's catching up on me.'

'You work too hard,' she murmured.

He stretched out a long arm. 'Come here.'

Zee knelt down beside him and Lorn raised his head, catching the beaded tip of one slender plait between his teeth. Tugging gently, he captured her, forcing her closer until she could feel the warmth of his breath caressing her cheek. He raised devoted fingers to her hair, stroking the heavy fall wonderingly, his eyes soft and serious. Zee sought to master her rising excitement, but it was impossible. As he trailed his fingers across the smooth line of her jaw she reached out a hand, running it over his moustache. The hair was thick, springing back like wire at her touch. Lorn parted his lips, pushing the plait free with the tip of his tongue before turning his attention to her fingers, licking and nibbling at them. His hand moved to the back of her head, pushing through the thick hair, dragging her closer. Dreamily she replaced her fingers on his mouth with her lips, and trembled as he laid siege to her mouth, playing havoc with her senses as the savage rasp of his upper lip burned into her skin. His desire strengthened. Half rising, he grasped her hips in his large hands and with one supple movement lifted her from the floor, steering her body on to his. Pulses throbbing like the husky twang of an electric guitar, Zee lay on top of him, revelling in the hard maleness of him. Her breasts were flattened against his muscled chest and she could feel the driving strength of his hips pummelling into her soft curves. Relentlessly a hunger began to gnaw inside her, matching her passion to his. His fingers strayed to her throat and the vee neck of her shirt. For a moment he was content to stroke the smooth fullness beneath the thin cotton, but then, impatiently, he thrust his hips, moving her sideways. Now she was wedged between Lorn and the back of the velvet sofa, and his hands were free to wander. They began a voyage of discovery every bit as thorough as the one his mouth had accomplished. Zee quivered. Every inch of her wanted to be caressed, to be kissed. Vaguely she wondered why she had never felt this craving to be fondled with Mike. Lorn slid open the buttons of her shirt and silkily brushed her skin. As his palms rotated on her aching breasts Zee made a sound at the back of her throat, a sound of need, of desire.

'You're made of satin, my darling,' Lorn muttered brokenly, his thumbs circling on the swelling slopes. 'I knew you'd feel like this.'

There was a sensuous brush of his moustache as he deserted her lips and slowly worked his way downwards, kissing and nibbling, flicking her trembling skin with the tip of his pointed tongue. His mouth was hot and avid, burning into her throat, the hollows of her shoulders. As he reached the fragrant valley between her breasts a wave of sweetness broke over her, and she clung desperately to him, her hands dragging aside his sweatshirt until she was free to explore the curling mat of golden hair on his chest.

'God!' Lorn groaned huskily, grinding her hard against him. He stretched his fingers across her hips in the clinging jeans, probing and caressing the curves.

Zee heard a wail. Successfully spurning it, she rubbed her half-open mouth against his chest. The tanned skin smelt muskily male. The cry came again.

Lorn heard it too. 'That damn baby!' he complained, as Zee pushed herself up on to her arms above him.

'I'd better go and see what's wrong before he wakes Emma,' she said reluctantly.

Taking a deep breath to gain a measure of control, Lorn attempted to focus on his wristwatch. He blinked. 'Your sister and her husband will be home soon, I suppose—I suppose I'd better go.' Raising his head, he kissed one perfect round breast.

Zee staggered from him, fastening her shirt. It was an effort to stand upright in the confused aftermath of Lorn's lovemaking. She had never felt so aroused as she was now. Why hadn't it been like this with Mike? she wondered. When Lorn pushed himself up into a sitting position she noticed a fine sheen of sweat on his brow.

He took another shuddering breath. 'Perhaps we

ought to feel grateful for teething babies,' he said thickly. 'But I didn't want to stop. I *don't* want to stop, my darling. I ache for you.' He rose to his feet and held her against him, burying his face in her hair.

'I know,' she murmured.

'I want you so much, but we must do everything properly. It must be all or nothing for us,' Lorn said quietly.

The words sounded like a warning and Zee glanced up, puzzled, but as his mouth descended again she forgot what she had been about to say beneath the sweet torment of his kiss.

'No. No more,' he groaned, loosening his grip. He shook his head, blond strands falling across his brow as he tried to clear away the desire which had begun to claim him again. 'Where did I put my shoes?'

They were under the settee and when he had slipped his feet into them he walked with her into the hall. He collected his sheepskin coat and shrugged it on. Gordie's cries were intermittent now. An icy blast rushed in as Zee unfastened the front door.

'Until Heathrow, my darling,' he said, kissing her goodbye.

'Until Heathrow,' she echoed.

Life without Lorn was tedious. She missed him striding around, barking into the telephone, dictating at breakneck speed, arguing, planning and organising. How he had managed to become an integral part of her existence in such a short time defied explanation, but he had. Without him Zee felt as though she was adrift in a small boat, with only one paddle. Bracing her shoulders, she convinced herself it was a temporary reaction. He had provided a welcome breath of professionalism, and that was *really* what she missed, not Lorn himself. Once she was back in London, following her chosen career, natural ambition would begin to assert itself again and she would feel whole. Or so she presumed. . . . Her feet were beginning to itch for the hustle and bustle of city life.

For whatever reason, the next two weeks dragged. Work on the alterations had started at Greenan Towers, but as everything was already organised, there was little to do. All that was necessary was to keep an eye on progress. Everything was under control—Lorn's mixture of ultimatums, threats and orders had seen to that. The workmen referred to him in awed tones, but religiously kept to his instructions. Even Mr McCrimmon's original assessment of him as a 'cocky London upstart' had softened, and he was now hailing him as their saviour. Zee was not so sure. If the hotel didn't show a profit by the end of twelve months she knew Lorn would not hesitate in advising Mr Edgar to close it down.

Zee began her training sessions, and was delighted by the instant results. Previously everyone had worked without guidance, in a vacuum, but suddenly the atmosphere had changed as the staff were melded into a team. There was a community feeling of pulling together. Aileen washed the dye from her hair and had a perm. Old Jimmy pottered in the garden on fine days and even carried one or two suitcases. For the first time in years the filing system made sense. Zee happily noted the improvements to tell Lorn, and as the days passed she found herself growing more and more impatient to see him.

'Habsah says you can stay for as long as you like,' Carol reported, reading the airmail letter which had arrived on the mat. 'And will you take her some photographs of Emma and Gordie?'

'The two most beautiful children in the world,' Zee teased. 'How could I refuse?'

'If I write out a list, do you think you could bring back a few things?' Carol pleaded.

'Such as?' She knew Carol's lists of old. 'I'm only taking one suitcase, so I don't intend to stagger back with lengths of batik, or bags of *ikan bilis*, pineapples or lifesize wooden carvings.'

Her sister laughed. 'Lorn has plenty of muscles, you can speak nicely to him.'

Eyes searching the crowds, Zee waited in the queue at the
check-in counter. Tall and slender in a zipped
burgundy-coloured flying suit, she was attracting
appreciative glances and by-passed them all. Where was
Lorn? He had blithely said they would meet at Heathrow,
but the airport was a vast complex, handling thousands of
daily passengers. Her brows met in anxiety. They could so
easily miss one another. Even the jumbo jet which would
fly them to Malaysia carried hundreds of people.
Reaching the head of the queue, she lifted her large
leather suitcase on to the weighing platform.

'Either you have muscles like Muhammed Ali or
that's half empty,' the uniformed man behind the
counter teased. He was partial to redheads, and this
leggy thoroughbred was a beauty. Zee tucked a strand
of gleaming hair behind her ear.

'Half empty,' she confessed with a smile.

'Intending to bring home souvenirs?'

She nodded, then, as two large hands slid around her
waist, she stiffened, her heart beating like a caged bird.
When there was the intimate brush of a moustache on
her neck, she spun round delightedly.

'Lorn! I was wondering where you were.'

Giving her a short hard kiss, he turned to the man at
the counter. 'I'll have to go back to the end of the
queue, but would you reserve us two seats together,
smoking section.'

His natural authority made the man take notice.
'Yes, sir.'

After Lorn had checked in his luggage, they took the
escalator up to the international passenger lounge. Both
tall, both blessed with an unusual colour of hair, they
made a striking couple, but they were too wrapped up
in each other to be aware of the many looks which
came their way.

'I've missed you so much,' said Lorn, sitting close
beside Zee on the padded bench. The hard feel of his
thigh against hers was disturbing, and as he slung his
arm along the backrest and twisted a strand of her hair

around his index finger, her insides began to churn.

'How are you?' he asked. 'Tell me what's been happening.'

Ignoring the blue eyes drinking in her profile, Zee unzipped her leather shoulderbag and took out a notebook. 'Alterations on the bedrooms are well advanced. All the new washbasins have been installed and the painters are in,' she told him as she worked her way down the list. 'The new kitchen units have been fitted, plus king-size freezer and fridges.'

Lorn slid a finger beneath the collar of her flying suit and idly stroked the warm skin. 'Is Mrs Weir pleased?'

'Thrilled to bits,' Zee told him, fighting off her own thrill at his casual caress. 'You're Numero Uno in her estimation.'

'And what am I in yours?' he queried, his mouth slanting.

She wrinkled her nose, wondering what to say.

Tugging gently at her collar, Lorn coaxed her to turn her head towards him. 'I've missed you so much,' he repeated urgently. 'I've not been able to concentrate on business these past two weeks because I've been so busy thinking about you.'

A small coloured girl had wandered away from her family and now stood at Lorn's knee, listening to their conversation.

Zee smiled at her, grateful for a measure of diversion. 'I've missed you, too,' she admitted, wondering if she dare confess just how much, but discretion got the better of her. She flipped over the page of her notebook and continued. 'The filing system is up to date and the interior decorators have reported that the carpets and curtains should be delivered in a week or two.'

The little girl was a blatant audience, huge brown eyes trained on Zee's red hair. Sticking a finger into her mouth, she stood on one leg and waited for more.

'Isn't all this interesting?' Lorn teased, and the child giggled.

'And Aileen has had her hair cut and permed,' Zee wound up triumphantly.

He nodded. 'Good, she said she would.'

'You—you knew!'

A grin tugged at the corner of his mouth. 'I stroked her with my velvet glove, as you suggested. I hinted she would look cute with curls all over her head.'

'She does,' Zee agreed, eyes wide.

The little coloured girl performed a jig before them

'Very nice,' Lorn smiled when she had finished. Suddenly she was overcome with shyness and ran back to her family, where she continued to watch Zee and Lorn from the safety of a seat beside her mother.

'Aren't you pleased with the progress at Greenan Towers?' Zee asked when he made no comment. He was distracting her, his finger tracing love circles on her throat.

'Very pleased, but I'm even more pleased to be here with you. Have you heard of the Mile High Club?'

'I—er—yes,' she said, in a small wondering voice. She was well aware that to qualify for membership of the mythical club it was necessary to have made love in a plane at altitude.

Lorn chuckled at the startled expression stretching her eyes. 'Don't worry—I'm not suggesting we do anything unusual on a crowded jumbo jet! But next year I intend buying myself a small plane. Perhaps we could enrol then?'

He was joking—well, half joking, she qualified, swallowing hard and trying to think of a witty rejoinder, but without success. Following his train of thought had made her breath run out, and it was a great relief when the number of their light flashed on to the indication board and she could wriggle out of an answer.

A smiling steward ushered them into the first class cabin, directing them to their seats. 'Would you care for a drink once we're airborn, madam?'

'Dry white wine, please.'

The steward bowed his head in acknowledgement and turned to Lorn.

'I'll have whisky and water,' he instructed, his brisk manner indicating that he was a man in a hurry, a man going places. A man who knew exactly what he wanted.

Zee cast him a covert glance as she fastened her safety belt. His chin was dark with the faint shadow of stubble and there were smudges beneath his eyes.

'When did you arrive back from the States?' she asked.

Lorn ran a large hand across the roughness of his beard and grimaced. 'This afternoon. I came straight off the flight to meet you. I'd fully intended to go home first and change, but the U.S. flight was delayed. I was on pins all the way across the Atlantic. If I'd missed the connection with you I would have gone up front and crucified the pilot!'

She laughed, her face softening. 'You're overdoing it, Lorn,' she chided, putting her hand on his sleeve. 'You've spent most of the day in the air already, and now you're destined to spend all the night airborne. You'll be worn out by the time we reach Malaysia.'

'But I'm with you,' he said, as though that solved everything.

There was a low rumble as the jet engines sprang into life. The steward walked through the cabin, checking that seat-belts had been fastened and cigarettes extinguished.

'Tell me about your childhood in the tropics,' Lorn demanded. 'Tell me about your parents.'

Zee relaxed in the comfortable seat. 'My father was a young single man when he first went to Malaysia,' she explained. 'He was bright and breezy, an extrovert, I suppose, and he enjoyed the socialising that an expatriate lifestyle entails. It suited his personality. One year he came home on leave to Scotland and met my mother. It was a whirlwind courtship. She was carried away by his enthusiastic tales of his adventures abroad, and before she knew it, they were married and living in a wooden house in the middle of miles and miles of rubber trees.' As the plane began its race along the runway, Zee sighed. 'My mother was totally the wrong kind of woman to be uprooted. Her childhood had been sheltered. She was painfully shy, meeting strangers terrified her. Until she married my father she had always lived in the same small village where she knew everyone. Even going up to Glasgow for the day was a great excursion, so you can imagine the culture shock when she woke up to find herself halfway across the world. She never liked the climate, and she didn't care for my father's social whirl, so gradually over the years they began to lead separate lives. She retired to her bed, full of unexplained illnesses, all of a nervous origin, I suspect, while Dad retaliated by becoming more and more the life and soul of the party.'

The engines roared into their final thrust and the nose of the huge plane lifted, soaring up into the evening sky. After a few minutes it levelled off.

'How old were you when she died?' Lorn asked, smiling his thanks as the steward appeared with their drinks.

'Twelve.' Zee took a sip of wine. 'Until then Carol and I had gone to school in a nearby town, but it was obvious our secondary education would have to be in the U.K. Dad packed us off to boarding school. Poor Carol hated it, she broke her heart when she had to leave Habsah, our *amah*. I suppose basically Carol is a home bird, like my mother, that's probably why she married so young. She needs a nest of her own.'

'And you don't?' he queried, raising a brow.

'I don't like living alone very much,' she confessed, 'but I accept it. I loved boarding school from the very first day. I guess my motivation is different from Carol's.'

Lorn swirled the amber liquid in his glass. 'The nesting instinct is stronger than you realise. When you reach a certain age it tends to hit you.'

'Then I've not reached it yet,' she said defiantly.

'You will.' Lorn took a mouthful of whisky. 'Like you, I was very ambitious when I was twenty-five. I still am, but more and more I find myself wondering what the point is of all my success. So I have a luxury mews house and an expensive car—so what?' He shrugged broad shoulders. 'I sit alone in my house. I travel alone round the world. It doesn't add up to very much. My mother is the only person who truly cares about me, and as she lives in Denmark we don't get to meet too often. When I come across a family with small children, like your sister's, I realise just how much I'm missing out.'

'Then—then you'll have to find yourself a wife,' Zee returned, her mind racing. What gorgeous children she and Lorn could make together—tall and strawberry blond. Resolutely she kicked the idea away. Whatever was she thinking about! He had had time to work out his ambitions, she hadn't.

'Yes,' he agreed, smiling at her, 'I suppose I will.'

As the jet headed towards the east, the steward came forward to freshen their drinks.

'The name of the hotel in Malaysia is the Pantai Tropika,' Lorn told her, unfastening his seat-belt and reaching into his breast pocket for his cigarette case. 'It's run by a German couple, Claus and Renate Schmidt.'

Zee's head jerked round, sending the heavy wings of hair flying against her cheeks. 'Then what role am I filling as a translator? I can't speak German.'

'Oh, you can help with the tradesmen, if we employ any,' he said casually, lighting his cigarette. 'Though I doubt there'll be much to do. The hotel is only ten years old and is making a healthy profit.'

Zee rested her elbow on the armrest, chin on her knuckles, fixing him with her large green eyes. 'I'm here under false pretences,' she glinted.

Lorn grinned without shame. 'You were under false pretences at Greenan Towers, so what's the difference?

Besides, I reckon I'm allowed to indulge myself occasionally.'

'I'm classed as an indulgence!'

'Yes, ma'am,' he said, squeezing her hand.

Mentally Zee sidetracked away. It seemed safer. His intentions were suddenly too blatant, and she needed time to think them through. But not now, not while he was smiling at her, the groove in his cheek making her legs feel weak and wobbly.

'Speaking of Greenan Towers,' she gabbled, 'I'd forgotten to report that old Jimmy had been working in the garden. He's due for some praise on your next visit.'

Lorn flicked away ash. 'He'll be gone by then. I've instructed Edgar that he's to be retired.'

Impotently anger swelled inside her. She had forgotten his implacable business tactics.

'You're a real bastard!' she blazed.

'Yes, I am, aren't I?' he said, examining the tip of his cigarette. Something in his voice quietened her. Suspiciously she watched him. His eyes were hard, full of hurt.

I must tell her, Lorn thought. His throat muscles were stiff, aching. He swallowed. She must know and better now before we go too far. But I've already gone too far, he realised grimly. I'm already in love with her. He moistened his lips with his tongue. If she leaves me, she leaves me, but, *dear God*! please make her stay.

After a moment he spoke. 'You're right. I *am* a bastard. I'm illegitimate.'

CHAPTER FIVE

His composure slipped.

'It's not important,' said Zee, wanting to take him in her arms and soothe away his pain.

The moment of vulnerability vanished as quickly as it had appeared. 'I agree.' Lorn thrust the thick fall of fair hair from his brow. He was back in control. 'Most of the time I don't give a damn, but the past has an uncanny knack of sneaking up and hitting you below the belt when you least expect it. When all's said and done we're only products of our pasts.'

'I suppose so.'

'We are.' His tone was aggressive, allowing not one iota of doubt.

Zee moved her shoulders. 'As far as I'm concerned, you're *you*. I don't give a toss about your parents.'

He raised his head and studied her, narrowing his eyes as he searched her expression. 'You're sure?'

'I'm sure.'

'Perhaps *you* don't care,' he retorted, 'but there are plenty who do. Society pretends to be fairminded, but when the crunch comes it's as bigoted as hell.' He took a ragged gulp of whisky.

'People like that are in the minority,' she insisted. 'I'm surprised you take any notice. Just tell them to clear off.'

Lorn gave a half smile. 'I usually do, though not so politely, but every once in a while something happens to wound me.' He stared past her through the cabin window where stars twinkled in the black satin folds of the night. 'Andrea terminated our engagement because I'm illegitimate.'

'She must have been mad,' Zee retorted. 'What difference does it make?'

Lorn pursed his lips. 'When I first told her, she laughed it away. We became engaged and her parents were told. Heaven knows, I hadn't deliberately kept it a secret from them, it had just never cropped up before—you don't drop references to your bastardy into the after-dinner conversation. I suppose I presumed she'd mentioned it to them, but it turned out that she hadn't. All hell was let loose!' He took a slug of whisky, draining his glass. 'Andrea's parents considered themselves from the top drawer. Her father was a well-known barrister, and her mother worked on charity committees, arranging lunches and balls. It was the high society scene. At first they'd considered me quite a catch—rich young man, destined for greater things,' he said sarcastically. 'But that quickly changed. Andrea became stiff and formal, all the spontaneity disappeared. We had an almighty row.' Lorn shrugged. 'She was full of excuses—how we weren't really suited. How we came from different backgrounds. How we didn't have much in common. It was a pack of lies.' His nostrils flared in derision. 'What she really meant was that it was too embarrassing to have a bastard for a husband. It wasn't socially acceptable. Afterwards she had second thoughts. She bombarded me with tearful telephone calls and apologetic letters, but it was too late. I wasn't going to forgive her.'

Zee frowned. 'Have you seen her since?'

'No.' A hard hand sliced through the air with merciless finality. 'I cut her out of my life.'

His tone made her shiver. Lorn would never allow anyone to make mistakes.

'But—but you didn't immediately stop loving her?'

'No. It took me a long time to pick up the pieces, but I succeeded in the end.' His face cleared and he smiled. 'I had a lucky escape.'

Tropical sunshine streamed through a gap in the heavy floral curtains. In sleep, Zee turned on the pillow, catching the slanted beam full face. Slowly she began to

surface, rubbing her eyes, squinting into the glare until
she had the sense to roll aside. She fumbled for her
watch on the bedside cabinet. Half past two. Breakfast
and lunch had come and gone.

It had been after ten the previous evening when they
had arrived at the Pantai Tropika Hotel. On the fifteen-
hour flight from London they had both managed a few
hours' sleep, but it had been shallow and fragmented.
There had been a tiresome wait at Subang Airport,
which served Kuala Lumpur, as they changed planes.
The second flight, this time in a twin-propellered thirty-
seater craft, had been eastwards across Peninsula
Malaysia to the small port of Kuala Kuning in the
north. A courtesy car had collected them from the tiny
airstrip and taken them to the hotel on the outskirts of
the town. Worn out by the long journey, Zee had been
too numb to pay much attention to her surroundings.
All she had cared about was sleep, and after the brief
formalities of registering, they had been shown to their
rooms. Saying goodnight to Lorn, she had turned away
into her bedroom next to his, and wearily undressed.
Within minutes she had been fast asleep.

Now she slid from between the sheets and walked
into the bedroom. Reaching up, she switched on the
shower and stepped beneath it, soaping away the last
remnants of tiredness. The splash of water, pounding
like rain on her naked skin, was invigorating, but the
cold wasn't a shivering cold, it was lukewarm. It always
was in the tropics. She smiled at the remembered
sensation, hugging her arms around her. It felt so good
to be back in Malaysia, her second home.

After shampooing her hair, she slipped on a loose
white cotton sundress trimmed with broderie anglaise,
and began to unpack. There was no sound from next
door. Perhaps Lorn was still asleep. He certainly needed
the rest. She didn't know how he had managed to cope
with their long journey, on top of his American flight.
True, he had been pale beneath his tan and there had
been a network of tiredness lines around his eyes, but

he had still managed to snap out instructions to porters and booking clerks with his usual alert authority.

Her unpacking completed, Zee slid aside the glass door and stepped out on to the balcony. Her hair was damp, neatly combed behind her ears, but ten minutes in the sun's rays would dry it to polished copper. Two gaily striped cushioned chairs, a low table and an array of pot plants filled most of the small balcony. She paused, resting her elbows on the perimeter wall as she inspected the view. Her room was on the first floor of the two-storey building. The hotel was L-shaped, most of the bedrooms on the shorter span, while the main section contained the reception lobby, restaurants, shops, conference room and other sundry offices. To Zee's right was a silver-white stretch of beach and the blue, blue sea. She had forgotten how vivid colours always appeared in the tropics. Below was a wide lawn and recreation area, badminton nets set out to one side. Sprawling bushes of pink and purple bougainvillea were interspersed with white frangipani, and in the distance was a swimming pool, sparkling in the bright sunshine. There was a kiddies' paddling pool beyond it, and faint joyful shouts from children splashing in the blue waters travelled to her. Zee raised her face joyfully to the sun, absorbing the glorious heat.

'Careful you don't get burnt!'

She whirled round. 'Lorn! I thought you were still asleep.'

He slid the glass door closed behind him as he came out on to his balcony. 'I was, until ten minutes ago.'

He had recently showered, his blond hair damply dark, brushed back from his brow and his jaw freshly shaven. A white towel was knotted around his waist. Zee's breath caught at the sight of his gleaming torso.

'Did you sleep well?' she asked, forcing her eyes from the mesmeric pull of his nakedness.

He yawned. 'Like the proverbial log, but I dare say jet-lag hasn't finished with me yet, or you. I suggest we skip work for a couple of days and give ourselves a chance to recover.' He eyed their adjoining balconies. There was an eighteen-inch gap between them. 'I'm coming over,' he decided, spreading a large hand on the wall on his side, to provide necessary leverage.

'Be careful,' she warned, but her words were superfluous, for Lorn vaulted easily over the low division. He studied her for a moment, then put his hands on either side of her head, drawing her to him. His mouth swooped down. There was the intoxicating thrill of his moustache, the pressure of his lips. He tasted of toothpaste, freshly minty. Involuntarily Zee slid her arms around his waist. The living gold beneath her touch was warm and smooth. His kiss deepened.

'Don't forget the spectators,' she said, a little unsteadily, holding herself apart.

Lorn threw a look at the green lawns below where holidaymakers chatted and dozed in the sunshine. 'Nobody cares.'

'I thought I was here as your secretary?' she asked archly.

'At the moment the management think we're on holiday,' he muttered, unhooking her hair from behind her ears and smiling at the polished sheen.

Zee shifted uncomfortably. 'Do we have to pretend, Lorn? Can't we be honest and tell them from the start why we're really here?' she pleaded. 'You said yourself the hotel was profitable. What's the point in snooping around?'

He released her to lean back against the wall, folding his arms. 'You make it sound so underhand,' he complained, his eyes hardening. 'It isn't. If I tell the Schmidts I'm here at Edgar's request then obviously they'll lay out the red carpet, and I don't want that. If I'm to do the job properly I must see the genuine day-to-day operation of the hotel.'

'And what will the Schmidts think when you reveal that our true purpose has been to spy on them?' she flared.

'I don't give a damn what they think,' he growled

through gritted teeth. 'My sole concern is to make sure the Devenay chain prospers.'

'So individuals count for nothing!' Her thoughts raced back to Greenan Towers. 'Just like old Jimmy.'

'Be realistic, Zee. He should have been retired years ago, he's worse than useless.'

Secretly she admitted that was the truth, but she wasn't going to agree with Lorn.

'What about Mr McCrimmon, and Heather, and Mrs Weir?' she continued wildly, temper spurring her on. 'What will they do if Greenan Towers closes?'

Lorn spread his hands at his waist and glared at her. 'Don't be so bloody emotional!' he ordered. 'Mc-Crimmons's had a lifetime's free meal ticket, he's not entitled to more. And as for the rest of the staff, I'm sure they'll find alternative work.'

Zee stuck out her lower lip like a spoilt child. 'Well, it doesn't seem right,' she said lamely.

'I'm the good guy, Zee, not the bad one,' he told her. 'If you take the trouble to read the annual reports you'll discover that five years ago the Devenay chain was really in the—really floundering. Profits were at an all-time low. That's when I laid it on the line to Edgar— either he allow J. & M. Consultancy to become involved, or he accept that within twelve months he would be damn near bankrupt.'

'Are you a friend of Mr Edgar's?' she asked. The relationship between the two men continued to puzzle her.

'Sort of,' he said curtly before continuing. 'Clive started with the London hotels, while I concentrated on the States. By the end of twelve months profits were already on the upward curve. Last year gross turnover was the highest for several years. We've only had to close two hotels. One was in a Washington suburb which was originally high-class, but had deteriorated over the years until it was almost a slum. Selling up was the only remedy. The second was in Los Angeles, a factory had been built close by, so obviously that had little future, either.'

She noticed both hotels had come under Lorn's jurisdiction, not Clive's.

'And the third to close will be Greenan Towers?' she asked in a strained voice.

He sighed. 'I don't know yet, Zee, but as long as McCrimmon's in charge there doesn't seem to be much hope.'

'Then why don't you go ahead and sack him, too, like Jimmy?' she taunted.

'I probably will.' He stretched out a foot and rubbed his bare toes across hers. 'Don't let's argue,' he coaxed. The hypnotic charm of the deep groove in his cheek worked its magic and despite herself Zee's temper faltered.

'Shall we have a dip?' he suggested, scanning the swimming pool in the distance.

'Why not?' she agreed, conceding defeat. 'I'll meet you in the corridor in five minutes.'

Succumbing to drowsiness, Zee lay on her stomach on the padded lounger. Although she was in the shade of a palm and the late afternoon sun was beginning to dip in the sky, the air still felt like warm velvet on her limbs. Lorn was in the pool. After a swim they had sunbathed, making idle conversation as time drifted happily away. Resting her chin on her hands, she looked across at the sparkling water. Lorn stepped up on to the springboard. A short run, followed by a neatly executed dive, fair head tucked between muscular arms. He cut down through the water, a bronzed shape gliding, then surfaced, flicking his head sideways to swing the wet hair from his eyes. When he saw she was watching, he grinned, raising a hand in salute.

She waved back. All afternoon her eyes had been irresistibly drawn to him, and not only hers. There had been other interested female glances as Lorn swam up and down the pool, first doing the crawl then breaststroke. Tall and lithe, he cut a virile figure in the brief navy trunks, his pale hair shining in the sunshine. He dived again.

'I don't know where you find the energy,' Zee said in mock complaint when he returned to her side. Water coursed down his dripping body, trickling across the flat stomach, the firm thighs. He picked up a towel to rub his chest. Zee watched as dark damp hairs were dried into spun gold. She was filled with an urge to touch them, to run her lips across the springiness, to bury her nose in his clean male fragrance.

'I like to keep fit,' he smiled, his eyes idling over the full curves scarcely concealed by the purple satin bikini. 'I could write a book on the variety of hotel pools I have swum in.' He inspected the waterproof watch on his wrist. 'Shall we have dinner early this evening? I'm starving!'

Zee sat up to reach for her beach bag. 'So am I. I'll go up and shower.' She fingered her hair. 'I suppose I'd better have another shampoo to wash away the chlorine, but I'll be as quick as I can.'

'Fine. While you're doing that I'll go and find myself a drink in the bar. I'll meet you there.'

She pushed her bottle of tanning lotion and dark glasses into her bag. Slinging her towel across her shoulder, she stood up to join him. He took hold of her hand as they made their way upstairs.

Smiling goodbye, Lorn turned into his room. He stripped and switched on the shower. God! he thought, how am I going to keep myself under control? All afternoon I've been wanting to take her in my arms and make love to her. Steady, boy, he remonstrated, adjusting the dial to cold, don't rush things. You've only known each other a month, and half of that doesn't count because you were apart. He closed his eyes and leant against the tiled wall. But I love her, he muttered, I love her, I goddamn *love* her.

She heard the slam of his door when he went downstairs to the bar. Her hair was still damp, but it began to dry as she dressed and made up her eyes. The door to the balcony stood open, tropical warmth surrounding her. Later the door would be closed and she would switch on the air-conditioner to ensure the room became cool enough for an easy sleep. Happily relaxed, Zee examined herself in the full-length mirror. Already the sun had brought a glow to her skin. Being a redhead, she never tanned deeply, but the faint shimmer of colour was attractive. Her chiffon dress, in riotous shades of pale copper and scarlet, was strapless. The tight elasticated bodice outlined the tilted lines of her breasts and her slender waist, while the full skirt swirled around her legs. She slipped on high strappy sandals. Thank goodness Lorn was so tall! When she had dated Mike she had often worn lower heels in order not to equal his height, but her strappy sandals felt far more glamorous.

Her make-up was quickly accomplished. Taupe shadow on her lids and three careful coats of dark mascara, finishing with a touch of glosser on her full lips. For a few minutes she stood on the balcony and brushed her hair until it was dry, then plaited two fine plaits, fastening them with copper trinkets. Now she was ready. Locking the door behind her, she made her way downstairs.

The bar was decorated in the pseudo style of a fisherman's cabin. Coarse nets hung from the walls, and blue and green glass buoys provided a dim light. Pine planking, sanded to the colour of flax, covered the floor, while rounded rattan chairs with squashy blue and green patterned cushions were dotted around low tables. Exotic tropical foliage tumbled from a variety of lobster baskets and barrels, and the leafy green and yellow tendrils of money-tree plants clung to wooden beams which supported the low ceiling.

Zee paused for a moment, allowing her eyes to adjust to the gloom. Despite the early hour, several tables were already occupied, and a row of customers lounged against the brass-sheeted bar counter, sipping drinks.

Taking a hesitant step forward, she scanned the room, but without success. More tables were concealed from her view at the far end of the room, and as she caught sight of Lorn in the far corner, her heartbeat quickened. His chair scraped on the wooden floor as he rose to greet her. She hid her surprise when she realised he was not alone.

'May I introduce Renate Schmidt?' he asked, pulling Zee close, his arm resting with easy familiarity at her waist. 'Renate is the manageress of the Pantai Tropika.'

Zee smiled at the ebony-haired young woman relaxing in a chair pulled close to Lorn's. Renate Schmidt was not at all the homely *hausfrau* she had expected. Rapidly Zee became aware that she was being assessed, as shrewd black eyes travelled over her, noting her age, her looks, her style. The elegant creature even inspected her ringless fingers, and Zee felt a prick of hostility at the blatant dissection.

'Zee is my—my. . . .' Lorn continued his introduction. He paused, and for a split second she wondered if he would be honest and reveal that she was here as his secretary, and that his true purpose at the hotel was on a consultancy basis. She held her breath. There was a moment of tension which Mrs Schmidt seemed to catch, for a manicured hand moved to toy with a jade drop at her throat.

'Girl-friend,' he finished, with a small smile.

She was unable to decide whether the German woman was pleased or disappointed at his words, but a shadow flickered momentarily across the carefully painted face before she patted the vacant seat beside her.

'Do sit down,' Renate entreated, raising a slender arm and snapping her fingers at the Malay barman. Immediately he abandoned the glasses he was polishing and came to their table. As Lorn ordered drinks, Zee allowed herself a discreet appraisal of Mrs Schmidt. She could be no more than thirty, a *femme fatale* confident of her own allure. Drifts of jet black hair curled in profusion around her oval face which was flawlessly presented, dramatic dark shadow on her eyelids and bright red lipstick. Her crimson sheath dress had a plunging ruffled neckline which exposed milky white curves to perfection.

'Lorn tells me you have travelled directly from the U.K., *ja*?' she commented in faintly accented English. Her voice was pleasingly low. 'What a very long way to come for a holiday!'

Zee looked down into her glass of wine. It bothered her that she was forced to take part in Lorn's deception.

'The journey was worthwhile, just to stay in such a pleasant hotel,' he intervened, coolly taking the ball from her court. She flashed him a look of gratitude.

'Thank you for the compliment, Lorn,' Renate purred, carefully adjusting her skirt to reveal two smooth knees and a tantalising hint of white thigh.

Zee watched the performance with surprise. First names were being bandied around with familiar ease and, the German girl's interest in Lorn was brazenly apparent. The fact that Zee, supposedly his girl-friend, was sitting beside him had been totally discounted. She wondered if Mr Schmidt was aware that his wife was in the habit of chatting up strange men in his bar, for it was apparent Renate had had plenty of practice. She was completely relaxed, her hand straying now and then to touch Lorn's arm as she emphasised a particular point. Zee banked down a flare of irritation at his nonchalant acceptance of the flirtatious display. She had to acknowledge that her reaction was unreasonable. Lorn was a good-looking and virile man. His past must have been littered with amorous women, married as well as single, but even so his willing participation in Renate's lighthearted banter annoyed her.

'Is Mr Schmidt off duty this evening?' Zee heard herself asking, the temptation to remind Renate of her marital status proving too great to resist.

'Claus is supervising a private dinner in one of the convention rooms.' The reply was serene, no flickers of guilt. 'He'll be tied up until ten, but perhaps we could all have a drink together afterwards.' She turned to Zee and smiled. 'He's rather fond of redheads.'

Her blood chilled. If she had caught the correct innuendo, Renate was pairing them off—Zee and the unseen Claus, herself with Lorn. Perhaps the Schmidts had one of those 'open' marriages she had read about in magazines, where each partner was free to indulge in extra-marital affairs.

'Not me,' she said hurriedly, trying to appear cool and poised. 'I shall be going to bed early tonight. I'm exhausted.'

'Jet-lag has caught up with me, too,' Lorn agreed.

She threw him a searching glance. Was he wary of Renate's freewheeling attitude, or was his tiredness genuine?

'Tomorrow evening, *ja*?' Renate asked, in a light tone threaded with steel. 'I'll tell Claus, he'll be delighted.'

Zee had a fluttery feeling in her stomach. She was getting into something dangerous, something she didn't like.

'Fine, we'll look forward to that,' Lorn replied, smiling at her as he carelessly compromised them both.

She bit down on her lip. His bland agreement to the drinks date was infuriating. She had no wish to be paired off with Claus Schmidt, and more to the point, she didn't want Lorn to become friendly with the glamorous Renate. Not at all. Cold claws of jealousy ripped at her heart, bringing gooseflesh to her spine. She didn't want to share him. Her fingers tightened around the stem of her wine glass. Don't be foolish, she told herself, Lorn doesn't belong to you, Not yet. Though he so easily could. She admitted, for the first time, that she was halfway in love with him, and every look, every touch, told her the feeling was reciprocated. In turmoil, her mind raced. If she allowed their relationship to progress she would be trapped. Keep it light, she cautioned herself, remember your career, and remember what happened with Mike. . . .

But it could be different with Lorn. Could it? a loud voice in her head jeered sarcastically. Be realistic, Zee. Haven't you always planned to make your own way in the world? You don't want Lorn, at least not on a permanent basis, so why not stand back and leave the field free? Now her blood froze. No, she thought, I can't do that, not yet. She forced her attention back to the conversation.

'Do you have many private functions?' Lorn was asking.

Renate twisted a glossy curl around her finger. 'The Rotary Club meets here each week,' she told him, 'and there are the usual local dinners and parties. Also we offer a special package for business conventions which is proving very popular.'

'You and your husband must be kept busy,' Zee inserted.

'My husband?' Renate tossed back the mist of black curls and gave a tinkling laugh. 'Claus isn't my husband, he's my brother.'

'Oh, I—I see.' Zee gulped down the dregs of her wine and turned to Lorn. 'Shall we go and eat?'

By the time their meal was over she had reconciled herself to the fact that Renate was unattached, and considered Lorn fair game.

'The manageress is very striking, isn't she?' she remarked, watching his reaction from beneath her lashes.

'She is, and very direct,' he grinned. 'She came over to my table and announced that as I was the best-looking man in the bar she would join me.'

The introduction might have surprised him, but Zee was aware he had not found it unpleasant.

'If you want it, grab it,' she said in a tight voice.

He ran a fingertip across the back of her hand and smiled. 'That strategy might be effective for casual pick-ups, but basically it has its faults. I'm glad you and I didn't meet in a bar. I'm grateful we have something more substantial to build on. We work well together, Zee, in more ways than one.'

The aching throb in his voice told her what he meant.

She raised her large green eyes. 'I know,' she said, 'but. . . .'

She didn't really know what she intended to say next. Perhaps that she didn't want their involvement to become any deeper? Perhaps that it was wiser to backpedal and revert to the boss–secretary relationship?

'But it's time we went to bed,' Lorn intervened, breaking her train of thought. He laughed when he saw the look on her face. 'Separately, at least for the time being,' he assured her. 'You look tired out, and I know I'm desperate for some more sleep.'

Together they climbed the stairs.

'Do you have an arrow on your ceiling?' he asked as she unlocked her door.

'A what?'

'An arrow. Honestly, there's one over my bed. This isn't some devious ploy to get into your room.'

He was at her shoulder as she snapped on the light.

He pointed upwards. 'There.'

A paper arrow bearing the word *'kiblat'* was fixed to the ceiling.

Zee chuckled. 'That's to show the direction of Mecca. Many Malays are Muslim, and the arrow shows them the way to face when they kneel to pray.'

'Ask and it shall be told,' Lorn teased, his eyes sparkling. 'I was very wise, bringing you along.' He pushed the door shut behind him. 'And as I'm in your room, by devious means or not, I might as well take advantage.'

He put out an arm and switched off the light. It was pitch black, the curtains drawn against the moon. Zee could hear the gentle chant of his breathing as his hands slid around her waist, clasping her to him. His sensuous kiss wiped away her tiredness. Now life pulsated within her, turning her veins to rivers of molten fire. She clung to him, absorbing the maleness of him, the contrasting textures, the moistness of his demanding mouth, the smoothness of his skin. As she slipped her fingers between the buttons of his shirt, she could feel his body heat. She tugged at the fastening.

'No,' he said, after a moment, his fingers capturing hers, holding them still. He took a deep breath. 'My resistance is low this evening, my darling,' he continued huskily. 'If we start I won't be able to stop, and now isn't the right time. We're both dog-tired.' Kissing the palms of her hands, he switched on the light. 'I'll see you in the morning.'

'I suppose there's no way we can escape Renate's invitation?' Lorn asked wistfully, the next evening.

It was after dinner, and they were strolling barefoot along the shore, hand in hand. Stars twinkled in the dark sky. Only the rhythmic wash of waves on the white-gilt sand broke the still of the evening. A perfect ending to a perfect day, Zee thought contentedly. They had taken things easy, rising late, enjoying a leisurely lunch, and then basking by the pool for most of the afternoon. Time had trickled by and they had been happy in each other's company.

'None,' Zee smiled, secretly pleased to hear the reluctance in his voice. 'I bet she has lookouts stationed at all the doors!'

He slanted his watch at the moon. 'Fifteen minutes to go,' he complained. 'It's getting to feel like the death sentence!'

Three times that day Renate had reminded them of the ten o'clock deadline. She had even appeared while they were at dinner, to instruct them to go through a door marked 'Staff' behind the reception counter.

'I don't know why she's so keen for *us* to have drinks with them,' Lorn grumbled. 'There are plenty of other couples she could ask.'

Zee knew exactly why. Renate fancied Lorn, it was as simple as that. Most of the other guests were married couples, single men were at a premium. Zee realised there would be only a handful of European males resident in Kuala Kuning, again probably married. Renate's main contact with eligible men would be at the Pantai Tropika, and that meant a time scale limited to the length of their stay. Zee and Lorn were booked in for two weeks, far longer than most, for Kuala Kuning was the kind of holiday resort people included on a high-speed tour of South-East Asia, spending only two or three days at each location.

Renate must have made an instant decision that Lorn was suitable and was now pulling out all stops to attract him. Opposition in the shape of an accompanying redhead did not appear to worry her. Zee frowned at the unflattering implication. Thoughtfully she walked beside Lorn, taking pleasure in the warm grip of his hand, the soft sensuous fall of fine sand between her toes.

'Can't we tell the Schmidts you're a consultant?' she pleaded. 'It's so two-faced to accept their hospitality when all the time they imagine we're *bona fide* visitors. It's cheating!'

Lorn halted. 'Heaven preserve me from persuasive women!' he sighed in mock despair.

Something in his voice made her spin to face him. 'You mean you'll be honest?' she asked. 'Oh Lorn, thank you!'

Impulsively she threw her arms around his neck and kissed him. She could feel him laughing, his mouth quirking beneath hers. His lips parted and the frivolity was replaced by a far stronger emotion. His hands slid upwards to caress her breasts, the heat of his fingers burning through the fine silk fabric as he gently teased the firm peaks into rigid knubs of desire. Bending his head, he moved his mouth from hers to blaze a fiery path along the rim of her jaw. Zee arched her back, joyously allowing him freedom to kiss the silken column of her throat.

'Lord!' he complained, as his hands and mouth met in the neckline of her dress. 'Couldn't you have worn something I could unfasten?'

She rubbed her forehead against his, laughing at his despair. 'I didn't anticipate this situation, Mr Jensen,' she teased, in a secretary-type voice.

'Next time be better prepared, Miss Robertson,' he retaliated, 'Otherwise I shall be obliged to release you from your duties.'

'Yes, sir,' she laughed, taking hold of his wrist and inspecting the heavy watch. 'We'd better walk back, Lorn.'

With a sigh of resignation he obediently steered her around in the sand. Beckoning lights of the Pantai Tropika shimmered in the distance. Zee leant against him, enjoying the feel of his arm across her back, the intimate touch of his hand resting on her hip. It took all her self-control to resist the urge to hurl herself back into his arms, but as they retraced their steps her pulses steadied to normality.

'I wonder where that came from?' said Lorn, as they drew level with an old fishing boat marooned half in, half out, of the water. Scoured by the sun and rain, the bleached wooden hull was holed in places, waves washing on to the lower deck.

'Vietnam, I imagine,' Zee told him. 'Habsah wrote and said that thousands of boat people had arrived in Malaysia after fleeing across the South China Sea. The authorities have set up refugee transit camps here.'

'And what happens to the boats? Are they left to rot?'

She shrugged. 'I don't know.'

Together they inspected the boat. Sand had drifted across the timbers, covering the corners of the deck. The boat was frail and alarmingly small. Zee shuddered at the mental picture of men, women and children crossing a wild and tempestuous ocean on its crowded decks.

'It seems such a waste, lying there,' Lorn muttered as they turned away.

Collecting their shoes at the edge of the lawn, they walked back into the hotel. Zee dusted down the skirt of her dress, smothering a knot of tension which was tightening her temples. She was confident she looked attractive. Her dress was a slim-line shift in brown silk with a fine gold stripe, the colour flattering her bright hair. Why then was she tempted to make some excuse and rush up to her room to re-check her appearance? She had no wish to impress Claus Schmidt and certainly none to compete with Renate. Or had she. . . .

'Welcome, welcome!' The door was flung open wide and Renate laid immediate claim, placing possessive fingers on Lorn's wrist and drawing him into the private lounge. She was wearing a black jumpsuit which clung like wet plastic, revealing all her curves and the fact that beneath it was nothing more than naked femininity. Zee smiled a polite greeting, receiving a brief flicker of appraisal in return before the darkly flashing eyes honed in again on Lorn.

'This is Claus.'

It was almost an afterthought. A tall young man, as dark as his sister, was standing by the window, a tumbler of whisky in his hand. In different circumstances Zee would have agreed he was handsome, and responded in kind to his friendly smile, but this evening she was acutely aware that his sole purpose in life was to keep her occupied.

'Good evening,' she said coolly.

Renate engineered the seating with consummate skill, and before Zee realised what was happening, she found herself and Claus in armchairs opposite Renate and Lorn, who were sat together on a black velvet settee.

'Have you had a pleasant day?' Renate asked silkily, leaning close to Lorn. Again the slender fingers were caressing his arm.

'We've spent most of it relaxing by the pool,' he replied, returning her smile with such ease that Zee wanted to murder him. 'And we've been eating too much of your delicious food. Zee has been encouraging me to try the local dishes. I'm becoming addicted to the seafood and the curries, but they're no good for the waistline.'

Ruefully he patted his iron-flat stomach, giving Renate the excuse to eye his physique'

'You're in perfect shape,' she murmured.

'If you wish to hire a car and explore the coast, it can be easily arranged,' Claus interrupted.

Lorn nodded a smiling acceptance. 'Thanks, but before we go any further I should explain the real reason for my visit to Malaysia. The Devenay management have engaged me as a consultant to improve their hotels. I'm here on business.'

Apprehension caught at Zee's throat and unconsciously she swallowed, leaning forward in her chair, waiting with bated breath for an indignant outburst. She wondered whether Renate's loving attention would drain away when she realised his deception.

Claus rose to his feet. '*Ja?* Sounds an excellent idea. I knew some of the other establishments had been revitalised and I was wondering if we would be given a turn. You must tell me how I can help you. Now, what will you have to drink?'

Zee's eyes widened. Mr McCrimmon had initially viewed Lorn's interference as the kiss of death, but Claus was making no complaint. Her gaze moved to Renate. The capturing fingers still rested on Lorn's arm, the dark eyes still devoured him.

As Claus mixed their drinks at the small bar in the corner of the lounge, Renate turned her attention to Zee. 'Are you here in a business capacity, too?' she asked.

'I'm Lorn's secretary.'

She wished like mad that she had the audacity to announce that she meant far more to him than that.

'Secretary?' Renate sucked at the word, liking it. A smile elongated her crimson mouth. 'I understand,' she murmured, sinking back into the soft upholstery, her thigh tight against Lorn's.

No, no, you don't! Zee wanted to scream, but the

moment had gone. In the other woman's eyes she had relinquished all claim to him.

'When do you wish to inspect our books?' Claus asked, returning with their drinks.

Lorn took a swig of whisky. 'There's no rush—some time in the next few days. From what I've already seen you run a highly competitive operation. I studied the accounts in London, and I'm full of admiration.'

'Profits should be even better this year,' Claus smiled, pleased with Lorn's words. 'The convention deal is becoming popular with businessmen as far away as Tokyo and Manila. We're booked up for months ahead.'

'Splendid!' Lorn nodded thoughtfully. 'I believe the plot beyond the swimming pool already belongs to the Pantai Tropika? It would certainly be worth considering an extension. I'm a great believer in forward planning.'

'Good idea,' Claus agreed.

'And I noticed a stretch of land on the far side of the hotel which is running wild. Do you know the name of the owner, and what price they would take for it?'

Adrenalin was starting to flow, changing Lorn into the brisk businessman. Unconsciously he edged away from Renate, leaning forward to speak with Claus, his interest centred on his ideas for the hotel.

'Who owns the fishing boat on the shore?'

Claus turned down the corners of his mouth. 'No one, I guess. The Vietnamese who arrived in it were dispersed to camps long ago. They're probably in the States by now. Why?'

'I wondered if it could be put to some use, perhaps as part of a children's adventure playground.'

'Or a bar,' Zee suggested out of the blue, her imagination leaping away. 'If the boat was refurbished it could be set on the lawn and surrounded by a cobbled patio. There could be displays of flowering shrubs, or perhaps a water garden, all spotlit at night, with coloured lights strewn around the hull. Drinks could be served from the deck and extra tables positioned on the patio. It would create an interesting feature, especially if you had a plaque on the side listing something of the boat's history.'

'That's a great idea,' Claus agreed enthusiastically, turning to her. 'The temperature is very pleasant in the evenings. I'm sure guests would relish having a drink in the open air. We do have an outdoor barbecue, but that's only once a week. A regular garden bar would be popular and it would release pressure from the drinks service indoors. At peak times the bar gets very congested.'

'Why didn't I think of that?' beamed Lorn, smiling at her. 'And if I decide to go ahead with an extension, another air conditioned bar could be incorporated.'

Enthusiasm sparked between the three of them as ideas were bandied back and forth. Claus supplied several suggestions of his own and these were discussed at length. Initially Renate adopted an air of interested participation, but as time went by her expression glazed and she paid little attention to the discussion. Instead she lounged on the couch, smoothing the tight jumpsuit over her curves and inspecting her lacquered nails.

'Good God, it's after midnight!' Lorn exclaimed at last, looking at his watch. He drained his glass. 'We'd better stop now. Let's allow ourselves a day for the ideas to gel, and then we'll get down to work.' He stood up, pulling Zee to her feet. 'You need your beauty sleep,' he grinned, noting the paleness of her complexion. 'You'll never be awake for that pre-breakfast swim we promised ourselves.'

When she slid aside the balcony door the next morning, a lithe figure was already pounding up and down the pool in solitary splendour. Zee marvelled at his energy and yawned. Fifteen minutes later Lorn knocked at her door.

'Hello lazybones,' he said, leaning against the frame, eyeing her trim figure in the white pants and sunshine yellow blouse.

'You're disgustingly energetic!' she retorted, poking him in the ribs. In blue jeans and white tee-shirt, he brimmed with good health.

'Grr!' he gave a mock growl and pounced on her, gathering her up in his arms and kissing her. Zee struggled, laughing as his hold tightened, but when his mouth parted on hers, all wish to free herself faded. As he roamed her mouth with his lips her body became pliant, moulding itself against his hard contours. Desperately her fingers lost themselves in the thickness of fair hair at the back of his head, and as his hand closed around her breast, she sighed.

There was a clearing of a throat, and a polite cough. 'Excuse me, Miss Zee.'

She swung round, tearing herself from Lorn's embrace. 'Yusuf!' she exclaimed.

The bedroom door had swung open and a Malay in his late fifties stood in the corridor, his swarthy face flushed with embarrassment at their ardour. He gave a shy smile and cast down his eyes. 'I'm sorry to disturb you, Miss Zee. The lady said to come straight up.'

'That's—that's all right,' she assured him, hurriedly grabbing what shreds of composure she could. 'Can I introduce you? Yusuf, this is Lorn Jensen. Lorn, this is Yusuf bin Abdullah. Yusuf was my father's driver for many years.'

'Thirty-two years,' the little man said proudly. 'Tuan Robertson was very good boss.'

'Lorn is my—my—er. . . .' Zee stopped, her hand to her mouth. She had been going to say 'my boss, too', but then she realised the devastating impact such words would have on Yusuf. He would be affronted, appalled to think she allowed her boss such familiarities. Malay culture demanded reticence between men and women, casual touching was taboo.

Lorn stepped forward. 'I'm her fiancé. Zee and I are going to be married soon,' he said firmly.

CHAPTER SIX

'OH yes, I understand now. Good, good.' Yusuf's embarrassment faded, to be replaced by satisfaction at the disclosure. Now he could go halfway to accepting why they had been wrapped in each other's arms, though he did not honestly approve. Such ardent behaviour between Malay couples would not be condoned, but he realised Europeans followed a different code of conduct.

'We're about to have breakfast, will you join us?' Lorn asked, ignoring Zee's startled confusion. His glib explanation of their status had been disconcerting, to say the least, and as she walked with the two men into the restaurant, her mind went on the rampage. Lorn had helped her out of one predicament, but into another. Yusuf would be bound to report to Habsah that he had met Zee's fiancé, and that could only result in awkward questions. And if the news ever filtered through to Carol. . . .

She cast Lorn a suspicious glance, but he was indifferent to her unease, chatting comfortably with the Malay. Perhaps her scepticism was unwarranted, but had he merely been helping her out of a tricky situation, or was there some ulterior motive? Experience had taught her that Lorn was not a man to waste time travelling down blind alleys. Everything he did had a purpose.

'After Tuan Robertson died, I returned to my family village,' Yusuf was explaining. 'It is thirty miles from here. Habsah wrote and told me Miss Zee was visiting a Devenay hotel in Kuala Kuning, so I made some enquiries, and here I am! I have come to invite you to my daughter's wedding.' He smiled at Zee. 'Seha is to be married next week. I would be pleased if you and your fiancé would attend.'

'That's very kind.' She glanced at Lorn, who nodded. 'Yes, we'd love to come. How old is Seha now? She was still a schoolgirl the last time I saw her.'

'She is nineteen, the last of my babies,' Yusuf told her with a sigh. 'All the others are married now. I am a grandfather several times.'

The water appeared with steaming plates of *nasi dadang* and glutinous rice. Lorn lifted a forkful to his mouth, touching it tentatively with the tip of his tongue.

'Do you enjoy Malay food?' Yusuf asked, smiling at his wary expression.

'I'm learning, thanks to Zee,' he grinned. 'But I must confess curry for breakfast does rather stretch my taste-buds!'

It was mid-morning when Yusuf climbed astride his motorbike and fastened the strap of his crash helmet under his chin, ready for the journey home.

'*Selamat jalan,*' Zee smiled a fond farewell. Reminiscing about the past had flooded her with happy nostalgia, and her only regret was that Carol had not been able to share the experience. Together she and Lorn waved goodbye and strolled back into the hotel.

'Thanks for rescuing me,' she said gratefully. 'Our fake engagement can be ended as soon as we've been to Seha's wedding.'

Lorn shrugged. 'If that's what you want.'

'Do you intend to work this morning?' she asked, noticing that his mood had changed. He had thrust his hands into his trouser pockets and was striding up the stairs two at a time, deep in thought. Automatically she followed him.

He shook his head, pausing to allow her to join him on the landing.

'I'll make a few notes, but that's all. I've decided to go ahead with the extension. Claus can organise some estimates while I'm here. The sooner work starts, the better.'

Zee opened her bedroom door. 'Shouldn't you

consult Mr Edgar before you make a firm commitment?'

'No, why should I?' He followed her into the room.
'Shall we have a cool drink?'

Without waiting for agreement he strode to the small
fridge and took out two cans of lager.

'You act as though the Devenay chain belongs to
you,' Zee complained, joining him on the balcony.

With strong tanned fingers he prised the ring pull
from the first can and handed it to her, then reached for
the second. 'It does, to a certain extent,' he said, sitting
down and stretching out long legs. 'When I told you I
was illegitimate I didn't tell you the whole story. My
father was Robert Devenay.'

She froze, the can stopping halfway to her lips.
'Robert—Robert Devenay?'

'That's right.' Brusquely he ripped away the second
aluminium ring. 'He left me some shares in the
company. Not too many, merely sufficient to allow me
a voice without granting any control,' he said bitterly.
'My father was a very astute character.'

'Then Edgar is your half-brother,' she said, grasping
the implications.

'Yes, and anyone less capable of running a successful
business operation I have yet to meet.' He took a swig
from the can, wiping his moustache with the back of his
hand. 'Edgar ignored my advice for years, but
eventually he was forced to face financial facts. If J. &
M. Consultancy hadn't stepped in there would have
been precious little future for the Devenays.'

'Are you on their board of directors?' Like a jigsaw,
the pieces were fitting into place.

'Not yet,' he replied cryptically. 'It's only since Clive
and I have worked miracles that Edgar has publicly
accepted he has a brother. Not that he shouts it from
the rooftops, of course,' he sneered, 'but at least he
admits we're related. That's something. He ignored my
existence in total when I was younger.'

Zee watched him over the rim of her can, hurting at

the hard pain in his eyes. Now she knew why he had felt so strongly about Heather and her baby—his first-hand knowledge of being born on 'the wrong side of the blanket' had added a searing edge to his condemnation.

'Was it—difficult, not having a proper family?' she asked haltingly.

He gave a humourless bark of laughter. 'Naturally. Other boys had fathers to fly their kites or take them to football matches, but all I ever knew was a man with a booming voice who flashed in from time to time bearing expensive toys. He didn't give a damn about me, it was my mother he came to see.'

'Why didn't he marry her?'

'Because every time he asked, she refused him,' Lorn said tightly, 'and I suspect that suited him just fine. At heart he was very conventional, concerned about his social status, not the type to deal lightly with the scandal of a divorce.'

'But why did your mother refuse him?' Zee asked, wrinkling her brow.

'Because Edgar's mother was an invalid, and my mother was too softhearted to take her husband away from her.' He gulped down another mouthful of lager. 'Robert and my mother met when she went to work for his family as an au pair. At that time his wife's illness hadn't been properly diagnosed, it was in the early stages. She just felt off-colour and needed help looking after her children. My mother had left school and wanted to improve her English, so she answered their advertisement. After a while Mrs Devenay's condition was discovered to be serious, and they knew she was destined to wind up in a wheelchair. I imagine Robert was broken up at the news, and as my mother was very pretty, and gullible, he turned to her for comfort.' His nostrils flared. 'Robert took advantage of her, and I was the result.'

'It takes two,' Zee said.

He glared at her impatiently. 'For God's sake! She was a young girl in a foreign country. *He* was a wealthy man of the world, and a good twenty years older. He wasn't a fool. He must have known from the start what would happen. All he wanted was a beautiful mistress. When his wife couldn't provide him with sex any longer he looked elsewhere. He had the best of both worlds, damn him! Everyone admired his selfless devotion to his crippled wife, while my mother and I were discreetly tucked away.' He stared down at the can in his hands. 'Talk about a little bit on the side!' he jeered crudely.

'Did Robert's wife know about you?'

He lifted a hand in a vague gesture. 'She must have done, though she never admitted it. When my mother discovered she was pregnant she left their employ and went to live in a house Robert provided. He asked her to marry him before I was born, but she wouldn't hear of it.'

'Well, he wasn't all bad, then,' Zee pointed out.

'He only asked because he was certain she'd say no,' Lorn retorted.

'Do you know that for a fact, or is it supposition?'

Irritably, he moved his broad shoulders. 'Supposition,' he muttered.

'You're biased.'

'Okay, so I'm biased,' he snapped. 'But the fact remains that they didn't marry. My mother felt that as Mrs Devenay's condition was worsening, and there were Edgar and his sisters to consider, Robert's first family had more need of him. I admire her, in a way. I dare say her priorities were right, though she was a fool to let Robert off scot-free.'

'How do you know he *was* let off scot-free? Isn't it more likely that he suffered too?'

'He never showed it,' he flared, eyes sparking dangerously.

'And do *you* show all your innermost feelings?' she asked.

'*No!*'

Zee spread her hands. 'So?'

'So perhaps I'm a little one-sided,' he admitted.

'Your mother must have loved your father very much, perhaps he was worthy of her love.'

'Perhaps.' His voice became suddenly gentle. 'She never asked anything of him. I suppose that's what true love is all about. Even when Robert's wife died and he was free to propose she refused to marry him immediately. She said a decent interval must be allowed to pass, out of respect. She was concerned about *his* reputation.' He sighed. 'Ironically, in that interval Robert died too, so she never did become his wife. Afterwards she returned to Denmark. Her only reason for living in England for all those years was to be close to him. He left her well off, so she doesn't have any money worries.' As Lorn crushed the empty can in his fists, the metal buckled. 'I'm sorry if I sound bitter,' he continued, making an attempt at a smile which didn't quite come off. 'Emotionally Robert didn't give me anything, but financially he was generous. He paid for my education, and when I did well he began to take an interest of sorts. He steered me towards a business course at university. He told my mother it was his intention I should play a part in running the Devenay empire, but I don't know if that was the truth. I was only twenty when he died. I was too young to care much about the long-term future, and I even considered selling the shares he'd left me and buying a flashy sports car and a flat.' He grimaced at the memory. 'Fortunately, I didn't. By the time I left Harvard I was chock full with ideas of how to revitalise the Devenay company, but Edgar held up his hands in horror. It was only my shares which gave me sufficient power to force him to admit that changes had to be made.' Lorn pulled down the corners of his mouth. 'Now he's so damn grateful he never questions anything I suggest, and he's begging me to become a director.'

'Will you?'

'Not yet. I've spent too many years dangling on his string, and now that the positions are reversed I'm enjoying watching *him* squirm.'

'You're deliberately making him suffer!' Zee protested, but she couldn't disapprove.

Lazily Lorn leant back in his chair, and rested his feet up on the table. 'Yes,' he agreed with a lopsided grin, and reached for her hand.

Over the following days he reached frequently for her hand, and Zee's reservations about becoming too involved were discarded in the exhilaration of working with him again. Claus made up an energetic trio and together they spent hours striding around the Pantai Tropika and the vacant land, discussing ideas for new schemes and alterations.

At first Lorn's concentration on business made Renate sulky, but when an unattached Australian oil man arrived, her interest shifted. Lorn seemed unaware of her switch of affections, he was too engrossed, sounding out tradesmen and discussing construction plans and delivery dates.

From time to time Zee acted as his interpreter, though most of the men they dealt with spoke adequate English. Lorn's requirements were always worked out to the last detail, and when he produced his plans expressions would light up, fingers would jab and his infectious enthusiasm would spread. Claus provided a typewriter and, at first, Zee had used his office, but after endless distractions she decided it was easier to work in her room.

'There,' she said triumphantly, ripping a long report from her machine. 'All finished, and not too many mistakes either.'

Lorn turned from the balcony door where he had been patiently waiting, smoking a cigarette as he studied the upside-down moon. It was almost ten o'clock. Tomorrow they were abandoning work to attend Seha's wedding. Zee had been eager to finish the report so that it could be posted off promptly to Mr Edgar in London.

Lorn walked over and stood behind her, reading the

paragraphs over her shoulder. 'Thanks, what would I do without you?'

'You'd use Miss Canning, I'm sure she's a far superior typist.'

He put his hands on her shoulders. 'Perhaps,' he agreed, close to her ear, 'but she doesn't taste as good as you.'

'How do you know?' she asked pertly. 'Have you ever kissed her?'

There was a deep male chuckle as Zee reached for an envelope.

'Good God, no! You should meet Miss Canning. She's a fifty-year-old harridan, with spreading hips and glasses. Her affections are trained solely on her cats and her mother, in that order.'

Zee twisted her head to grin up at him. 'I imagined your secretary would be a leggy, sophisticated lady,' she said in amusement.

'You are,' he replied, reaching down to claim her lips.

She knew she should push him away. Every night she found herself in his arms, and every night it was becoming harder to turn from his kisses and sleep alone. Thank goodness Lorn exhibited a measure of control. . . .

The depth of her desire frightened her, for after her experience with Mike she had decided that lovemaking was overrated. Now she knew it wasn't. Lorn's kisses created a desperate need for fulfilment, a need she had never suspected she possessed. All her common sense told her it was better to keep him at arm's length, but how could she listen to common sense when his hands were sliding down over her shoulders and his breath was hot on her neck? Whispering words of love, he nibbled at her earlobe, and as she closed her eyes a flood of desire swept through her, making her quiver with excitement. Clasping her shoulders, he pulled her upright. His knee jerked out and moved the chair aside, allowing him to pull her close against him. The hard muscles of his chest rubbed against her shoulder blades, and the thrust of his thighs was turning her blood to liquid gold.

'Lorn. . . .'

What had been intended as a protest emerged as a moan of desire. His hands were splayed on her hips, gliding her against him until the masculine angles of his body rasped through her thin cotton skirt. With a confident hand he slipped open the buttons of her suntop and eased it from her shoulders. Zee felt a rush of wanton delight at the firm touch of his hands on her naked breasts. Murmuring his pleasure into her neck, he stroked the silky slopes, and aroused salvos of erotic explosions deep within her as his fingers stretched to rub rhythmically at the jutting peaks.

'I love you, my darling,' he groaned huskily, his breathing deep and erratic. 'I want to strew orchids in your path, and ring bells, and swim naked with you in the moonlight.'

'Lorn, Lord!' she sighed, pulling at his shirt.

He took a step towards the door and switched off the light, then threw off his shirt as he rejoined her. Now the room was dark, only a silvery edge of moon lit his pale hair and moustache.

'I love you, too,' she murmured, running her hands across the warm width of his shoulders.

'Zee, I want you so much,' he moaned, sinking his head into the richness of her hair. 'Marry me, my darling.'

Dazedly she stroked the strong column of his throat and as her fingertips glided across his chest she felt him tremble. She wanted to kiss him—all over, every male inch of him.

'Marry me,' he implored, passion hardening his words. His fingers had deserted her breasts to spread at her waist as he regained a degree of control.

'Not yet,' she said, suddenly panic-stricken, remembering Mike. 'Not yet. Don't rush me.'

Lorn didn't seem to understand. He moved, his chest rubbing across the sensitive points of her breasts, and

Zee arched her back, thrusting herself further into his arms.

'But you love me,' he mumbled, kissing the base of her throat. 'So what do you mean—not yet?'

'I don't want to get married, not yet. I—I want to have a career,' she said weakly.

'But you love me,' he said again, holding her from him. 'That changes everything.'

Her face was in shadow. 'In some ways,' she agreed, swallowing. 'Lorn, let me explain.'

He stepped back from her as though she was red-hot. 'Oh no, no bloody explanations,' he growled. 'It's take it or leave it, sweetheart.'

Zee's nails bit into the palms of her hands. How many times had she listened as he had snapped out his ultimatums? Her temper blazed. He was glaring at her, refusing to listen to reason.

'Everything must be black and white for you, mustn't it?' she accused. 'You allow no grey areas for discussion.'

'What the hell is there to discuss?' he taunted, grabbing at his shirt and flinging it on. 'Either you want to marry me, or you don't.'

'I—it's not as simple as that,' she said in a small voice, watching with growing despair as he moved away towards the door.

'It is in my book,' he growled. 'Goodnight.'

He had gone.

Engulfed in a confusing mixture of frustration and misery, Zee stood stock still in the darkness, trying to make some sense of her feelings. She heard Lorn enter his room, and a moment later turn on the shower. Deliberately, although she was sweating, she refused to follow suit. The image of them both naked with only a wall separating them was too poignant to contemplate. Flinging off the rest of her clothes, she lay face down on the bed, biting at her knuckles. There's no reason to cry, she told herself. You should have realised this would happen. But despite the admonition, two diamond-bright tears brimmed and trickled down her cheeks. She reached for a handkerchief to mop her face. Lorn is upset, she reasoned in an effort to bolster her flagging spirits. Tomorrow he'll listen to my point of view, and he'll understand. But deep down she doubted that he would. Even if she tried to explain about Mike. . . .

Her mind veered. Surely Lorn didn't imagine her refusal had anything to do with his parentage? There was a sharp pain in her chest. No, no, he mustn't think that. She didn't care that he was illegitimate. It was unimportant. Impulse lifted her from the bed. She would go and see him now to explain, but remembering his mood her blood ran icy.

'No explanations,' he had barked, and in his black rage he was incapable of listening to reason. It would be futile to knock at his door, he would only send her away. Zee crawled back to bed. It was wiser to mentally prepare her case and talk to him in the morning.

But in the morning her first anxious look at his face told her he was totally unprepared to consider anything she might have to say. He had reverted to the formidable stranger who had complained loud and long about the faults of Greenan Towers, but this time it was she who had aroused his displeasure. His aloof manner was both intimidating and infuriating. Zee couldn't bear so many loose ends. Every fibre of her yearned to talk the matter out, to make him understand, but Lorn was having none of it.

'It's over and done with,' he snapped, when she started to blurt out her explanation at breakfast. 'I'm not interested any more.' His lips were clenched in a tight straight line.

'But, Lorn. . . .' she protested.

'*Shut up!*'

Holidaymakers at nearby tables lifted their heads at his biting words, forcing Zee to abandon her attempt. It seemed foolish to sour his mood even further. She decided to leave it for a day or two until he had calmed down, and then she would try again.

'It's a lovely day for a wedding, isn't it?' she babbled, gazing out of the window at the clear blue sky. When she realised how inappropriate her words were, she turned to stone.

'Yes.' Lorn's reply was gruff.

Keeping her head carefully bent, Zee took a mouthful of fish curry. Usually the spicy prick on her tongue delighted her, but this morning it tasted like straw. For the remainder of the meal they were icily formal, passing toast and marmalade to one another as though complete strangers. Perhaps, deep down, they were, she decided. It was only weeks since they had first met. Unhappily Zee stirred the spoon round and round in her coffee cup. Lorn hadn't believed a single word she had said about her wish to be free and follow her own career. But it was true, wasn't it? Don't start having doubts now, Zee, she warned herself. Learn from your experience with Mike. For a moment she wondered if it was only his clumsy unimaginative lovemaking which had made marriage seem such a poor deal compared with a career. Was she deceiving herself? Could she live happily without a man, and without sex? Lorn had given her a taste of the physical joys of love, and she wanted more, but did she want marriage? If only Lorn was prepared to discuss their relationship, but with typical male arrogance he expected her to blithely reject her plans and turn into Mrs Jensen, housewife. She tightened her lips. No way, she thought acidly.

After breakfast she went with him to reception, and waited as he arranged the hire car. Renate was attending to the formalities. Zee realised the woman's emotional antennae were finely tuned, for she seemed instantly aware of the coolness Lorn exhibited and launched into action. The Australian was forgotten as she treated Lorn to what Zee disdainfully considered an embarrassing display of wisecracks and double entendres. And when Lorn brightened up, and began to respond in kind, trading easy quips, she felt like kicking him savagely on the shins and storming to her room.

'See you this evening!' Renate carolled when the forms were completed. Her black eyes signalled all kinds of promises.

'Look forward to that,' Lorn grinned, dangling the car keys from his fingers.

Zee sat stiffly beside him, examining the road map on her knee. 'The first section is straightforward, but if we get lost once we leave the main road, don't blame me.'

'Naturally I shall blame you, who else is there to blame?' he said coolly, glancing back over his shoulder to check the way behind was clear for him to reverse from the parking space.

As he completed the manoeuvre and swung out on to the road, she covertly inspected him. Was he joking? It didn't seem likely, though his conversation with Renate appeared to have loosened him up a little. Be thankful for small mercies, she thought, but the irony was too great. Why should she need to thank another woman for cheering up her man. *Her* man? Her stomach turned to lead. That train of thought was fatal. She loved him, but she wasn't ready yet to be tied down to marriage. Not yet, but perhaps some time. . . .

The leaden feeling lessened. If only she could put Lorn on ice and retrieve him in ten years' time. Her lips twitched ruefully at the idea.

'What's the joke?' he asked, glancing at her.

The edge had gone from his coldness, so she decided to take a chance. 'I was thinking I'd like to put you in a deep-freeze and come back and collect you in ten years' time,' she quipped, her heart racing.

'It wouldn't work. By then you'll be so knee-deep in cats, and so bloody self-sufficient, I wouldn't touch you with a bargepole.'

'Thank you!' she said, deeply offended.

He surveyed the pinkness in her cheeks and the eyes trained carefully ahead. 'You had your chance, Zee.

Let's not resort to a post-mortem.' He stretched out a pacifying hand.

'Don't touch me!' she shrieked. The twisted command emerged as a plea.

'Okay,' he agreed quickly, too quickly, as he returned his hand to the steering wheel. 'It's wiser to keep everything on a platonic level between us.' He sounded as though he was trying to convince someone.

'Why don't you have a holiday romance with Renate?' Zee bit out, jealousy deepening the cat green of her eyes. 'She'd be delighted.'

'I'm sure she would.'

He appeared to giving the idea careful consideration, and Zee panicked.

'Not while I'm around,' she blurted.

'Why not?' He arched a blond brow. 'After all, you are only my secretary.

There was no comment she could make, for a painful lump stuck in her throat, keeping her mute. For a few miles they motored along in silence. It was definitely not a companionable silence, though Lorn's original forbidding expression had eased somewhat. She cast him a glance. The balmy breeze had flicked a few blond strands across his brow, and he raked them aside with tanned fingers. He was wearing the batik shirt she had chosen for him from the hotel boutique. It was in blue and white, teamed with navy hopsack trousers. It was open at the neck and in the vee she glimpsed glinting hairs, golden against the burn of his skin. The hand resting in her lap trembled, as she fought the temptation to run her fingers across the wide expanse of bronze flesh beneath the thin cotton.

Zee looked away, out of the window. The small town of Kuala Kuning had been left far behind, and now they were on the rural coast road. Bouncing unawares over one jagged pothole, Lorn was now alert to the dangers of damaged suspension, and was concentrating on the way ahead. A lone goat wandered out from the grass verge and he swerved, swearing softly. They passed fields of pineapple, neat rows of spiky plants basking in the tropical sun. Zee took a deep breath, some of her tension dissolving at the delight of being back in the land she loved.

'Malaysia has its own special fragrance,' she declared, stretching out her arms.

And, my darling, so have you, Lorn thought grimly. I want to bury my face in your skin and never come up for air. But what's the point? You don't want to be married, and I'm damned if I'm prepared to settle for less.

His fingers tightened on the wheel. 'Tell me the procedure for Malay weddings,' he demanded.

Zee's expression softened as she recalled local weddings she had attended as a child. They had been exciting spectacles of colour and music.

'In the past celebrations went on for days, but now they usually last for just two,' she explained. 'The private ceremony, legalising the marriage, takes place the first day, and the public ceremony, the *bersanding*, is on the second. A woman called the *mak andam* is employed to supervise wedding protocol. She bathes the bride in water and limes to symbolically purify her, and attends to her make-up and hair. Celebrations often take place in community centres, and two thrones are placed on the *pelamin*, the bridal dais, which is decorated with rich velvets and cloth of gold so that it looks like something out of the Arabian Nights.' She laughed, warming to her subject. 'Malays love vivid colours and display. Seha and her groom will have been photographed in a variety of gorgeous costumes. The outfits are hired, and can range from Javanese dress, Arabian robes, Japanese kimonos to traditional Malay, or even Western clothes. I don't think the interpretations are strictly correct at times, but it's a wonderful opportunity to dress up in sequins and lace and jewels, and be king and queen for a day.'

'Sounds like fun.' Lorn was visibly relaxing.

'It is. Everything is informal, the women prepare the

makan, the men gossip, old people snooze and the children run riot. Malays love children and they're never restricted from the fun.'

Her face fell as she consulted the road map. 'Can you drive slowly? I imagine we turn off near here.'

As he reduced speed, she caught sight of a coloured spray of bright baubles attached to a signpost, and her expression cleared. 'Left,' she announced, with a glimmer of triumph.

There was a succession of gaudy sprays marking the way, and after a few minutes' drive along a dusty track through the trees, Lorn pulled the car to a halt outside a large wooden building. Men and women in sarongs were milling around, some clearly spectators, but others with a more determined step, involved in the festivities.

'Miss Prim and Proper, but beautiful with it,' said Lorn, coming round to open her door. It was the first personal comment he had made all morning, and Zee perversely refused to meet his eyes as she stepped out onto the sunbaked earth.

'Something more revealing would have been in bad taste.' She glanced down at her long brown skirt and white Victorian ruffled blouse with its wrist-length sleeves, then pouted. 'But I'm becoming hotter by the minute. Don't be surprised when steam comes out of my ears!'

He squinted up at the merciless blaze of the sun, high in a cloudless sky. 'I won't. I can already feel perspiration trickling down between my shoulder-blades.'

Stiffly aloof, he waited for her to take the lead. She had wondered in the car if it was only imagination which made her think he was holding himself physically apart from her, for there had not been a single brush of his shoulder against hers, not the chance rub of his thigh. Now she knew. His withdrawal was complete. True, she had shrieked that he was not to touch her, but he needn't be so damned obedient! All or nothing, she thought bitterly, and now he was giving sweet nothing. But it wasn't sweet, it was sour.

She turned from him, in relief, as Yusuf hurried out from the hall, a wide grin creasing his brown face.

'Miss Zee and Mr Lorn, welcome.' He greeted them with the traditional *salam*, hands lightly touching theirs before returning to his breast, which meant 'I greet you from my heart.'

Discreetly, Lorn handed him a small packet. 'A gift for the bride and groom, from my fiancée and myself.'

The words slashed into Zee's awareness like cold steel. For a brief moment her gaze collided with taunting blue eyes, before she hurriedly transferred her attention to Yusuf as he shepherded her into the hall to meet his wife and other members of his family.

As was always the custom at Malay celebrations, the men were on one side of the room, the women on the other. With determined gaiety Zee allowed herself to be swallowed up in a sea of chattering women. Her memories of Yusuf's wife, daughters and daughters-in-law, were precarious, but she jabbered away in Malay, resurrecting long forgotten events from her childhood and catching up on all the events of the past five years. Deliberately she refused to acknowledge Lorn's existence, and when at last she could no longer bear to ignore him, she felt a stab of pique for he looked completely at ease. He was sat at a long trestle table, drinking iced lime juice and chatting comfortably with a group of male guests. His lack of Malay did not appear to be a stumbling-block, and there were chuckles of laughter from his companions.

When Seha glided to her throne on the *pelamin* at the far end of the hall, Yusuf came across and directed Zee to Lorn's side. She was acutely aware that the only reason they were sitting together was because they were Europeans, and peevishly she wished they could follow Malay custom and sit apart. The atmosphere between them was so highly charged she felt she would have had an electric shock if she had chopped through it with a knife.

'What a pretty girl,' Lorn drawled, as Seha and her groom sank down on their decorated thrones. In her bridal dress of black and gold, Seha had all the regality of a queen. A gold filigree crown nestled in her dark hair, and her large brown eyes were demurely downcast.

'What's happening now?' he asked. A group of chattering young Malays had approached the couple.

'They're trying to make the bride laugh, but she isn't supposed to,' Zee explained. 'She has to maintain a shy appearance. It indicates her state of modesty.'

'What are they saying?'

'Things like "be patient" and "happy landing",' she said tightly.

Lorn grinned, and his dimple flashed. His unexpected smile made her feel suddenly weepy and depressed. God! he was so attractive when he smiled. Although, to all intents and purposes, he was outwardly charming, she was unhappily aware it was a lacquer-thin charade. In Malay eyes, his decorum and dignified behaviour towards her was correct, but Europeans would have gained a totally different impression. Their conversation was stilted, their eyes carefully trained on anyone, anything, but the partner across the table. Some kind of engaged couple, Zee thought disgustedly, when we can't relax for a second.

Despite the colourful proceedings and the tasty food, time began to drag. The temperature was soaring, and the air in the hall was heavy, clogging her pores. A headache crept up her neck into the back of her head.

'It's like a furnace in here!' she complained, gazing at the blades of a fan circling inadequately in the ceiling above their heads. As soon as it was politely possible, she glanced at her watch. 'Do—do you mind if we leave now?' she got out jerkily. 'I'm feeling rather faint, it must be the heat.'

If Lorn thought there was an emotional reason for her excuse, he didn't choose to comment.

'Fine,' he agreed, rising. 'I reckon the temperature in here must be well over a hundred.'

She saw that his batik shirt was wet, clinging clammily to his spine, dark with sweat. They made their farewells, chatting with the bride and groom, and then to Yusuf, who pressed a gift into their hands.

'*Selamat jalan,*' he smiled.

'*Selamat jalan,*' replied Zee, waving goodbye as they walked across to the car.

'It's like an oven in here,' Lorn grumbled as he opened the door and hot air rolled out.

'You should have left the windows wound down,' she remarked cuttingly.

'*You* should have told me,' he retorted. 'Why didn't you?'

'I really have no idea, sir,' she flared, deliberately needling him. Her head was hurting, and she was hot and uncomfortable, and unhappy.

His eyes were gritty with violent irritation. 'If you say that to me just one more time, sweetheart,' he threatened. 'I'll—I'll. . . .'

'You'll what?' Zee challenged with false bravado.

For a few harrowing moments she thought he was about to mete out a punishment there and then, but he tightened his jaw and growled,

'I'll beat that backside of yours until it's red raw, so just shut up and *get in the car*!'

All thought of retaliation faded beneath the hostility of his look, and Zee walked round to her door. It was war. Easing his long frame into the vehicle, Lorn swore savagely when he touched the burning steering wheel. Zee ignored the oaths, she was too busy pretending that her skin was not in danger of peeling from her back from its contact with the plastic seat. Sitting still was purgatory. At first she was sure she was in danger of third-degree burns, but once she had coped with the initial heat, the agony lessened, and now she was bathed in sweat.

Lorn shifted, grimaced and swore again. Head down, Zee examined Yusuf's gift. It was a *bunga telur*, a hardboiled egg, nestling in a basket decorated with bright paper flowers. Lorn shoved his egg under the dashboard and started the car.

'Did you enjoy it?' she asked as they drove out on to the main road.

'Interesting,' was all he said.

Disconsolately she pulled the petals from the tiny flowers, allowing the breeze to whip them from her fingers. They passed kampungs and mosques, rice paddies and oxen-pulled carts, but this time the spell of Malaysia refused to work its magic. Although her skin was clammy with perspiration, inside Zee felt cold as ice.

'I'll ask Renate to book you a flight to Kuala Lumpur tomorrow,' Lorn announced as the hotel came into view.

'Tomorrow?' she squeaked, wishing she had had the strength to be cool and indifferent, but she hadn't. 'Why?' Suddenly she was in a blue funk. She didn't want to leave, to leave *him*.

'It'll give you more time with your friend. There's not much more to be done at the Pantai Tropika, I expect to be finished myself in a few days. If I need any typing done I can always ask Renate for assistance.'

Zee scowled. 'I'm sure she'll be delighted to give you a hand,' she muttered. And anything else you want, she added silently.

'You'll enjoy seeing your friend again,' he said, as though he was doing her a favour.

'Yes.'

At best it was a tepid agreement. She was damned if she would fall over herself with gratitude when they both knew he was only getting rid of her, clearing the decks before Renate came aboard. She struggled to concentrate on the facts. Lorn had proposed. She had refused. Where did they go from here? Precisely nowhere. So why was jealousy tearing painful strips from her heart, one by one? It was emotional torture, but as Lorn had said, she had had her chance. It was expecting too much for him to stick around. He wasn't the kind of man to cry into his beer. He had successfully chopped Andrea out of his life, and now it was her turn.

'Will you excuse me from dinner this evening?' she asked as they drove into the car park. Gradually she was gathering composure. 'I'll have something light to eat in my room, then I'll go to bed. My head is throbbing.'

Switching off the engine, Lorn turned to her and grasped her upper arms. 'Are you sure you're all right?' he demanded, anxiously scanning her face. 'You do look rather pale.'

'I'll be okay,' she lied.

The only trouble with me is a broken heart, Zee thought as she went into her room, and *I'm* the one who broke it. She peeled off the clammy long-sleeved blouse and then the skirt, dropping them on to the carpet. Once I'm away from Lorn everything will slot back into place and I'll feel better, she told herself, and wondered who she was kidding.

'Habsah! You'll have me as fat as a pig!' Zee protested as another delicious spoonful was added to the heap of prawns on her plate.

'Make you big and strong.'

She laughed. 'But I'm big and strong already!'

'Too thin,' the Malay woman deliberated, her brown eyes inspecting the girl opposite her. 'But much better already. When you arrive three days ago I think—poor Miss Zee, so pale, so tired, so thin. Now you much better. You need to eat proper meals.'

'Like this?' In amused dismay Zee gazed at the succulent prawns in their tangy sauce. She lifted her chopsticks obediently, knowing Habsah would not let her rest until the plate was clean.

'You need a husband to look after you, like Miss Carol,' the older woman decreed, ripping the shell from a prawn and nibbling at the pink flesh. 'You got no boy-friend? What wrong with you?' With typical directness she cut through social etiquette. 'Miss Carol tell me you come with a man to Malaysia—where he gone?'

'He's probably on his way back to London by now.' Zee's reply was tinged with wistfulness.

'Why you not bring him see Habsah?'

'We had a quarrel,' she explained, wiping sauce from her chin. 'Well, not exactly a quarrel. He asked me to marry him, and I refused.'

'You not love him?' The query was brisk. Romantic love was a strictly Western concoction. Privately Habsah felt it came low down the list after respect, mutual trust and more mundane financial considerations. It had been affection, not infatuation, which had brought Tuan Robertson into her bed. He had been a good man, she reflected.

'Yes, I love him.'

Habsah's brow creased. 'Then why you not marry him?'

'To tell the truth, I'm frightened.' Zee paused. 'I feel that he's rushing me, Habsah. You know how impetuous I've been in the past?' The Malay woman nodded. 'The last time I rushed into a relationship it was disastrous, so I decided to steer clear of involvements for a long time. But then Lorn came along. . . .'

'And?'

'And now I don't know what to do.' Zee sighed. 'I'm ambitious. I want to have a successful career, and not just live life through my husband.'

'He say you not work?' Habsah demanded, looking perplexed. Why did Westerners create such unnecessary problems?

'No-o. I don't really know what he feels about me wanting to work,' she was forced to admit. 'We never discussed it.'

Habsah cast her a scornful glance. 'Maybe he want plenty sons straight away?'

'I—I don't know.'

An incredulous tongue clicked against teeth. 'You don't know? You never asked him?'

'It—it all happened very quickly,' said Zee, but it sounded a weak excuse, even to her ears. Maybe Lorn hadn't believed what she had said about her need of a career, but equally she had no idea what he expected from married life.

'We didn't get around to talking it out,' she added lamely.

'Then what your problem?' the darkhaired woman demanded. 'Maybe he happy you work. Maybe he says sons come later.'

'Maybe,' Zee echoed.

Lorn's sons. . . . The image was unsettling. Zee turned over on to her stomach, resting her head on her hands. Although it was well into the early hours, sleep still proved elusive. She could see now where they had gone wrong, and was forced to admit it hadn't been all Lorn's fault. True, he had refused to listen to her explanations after she had turned down his proposal, but she had had plenty of time before that to sound out his views on marriage. Reluctantly she admitted she had been so set on her own plans for the future that she had never spared a thought for his. After her experience with Mike she had developed tunnel vision, blinding herself to her emotional needs and seeing the future in only one context—a career. It was safer that way. . . .

In retrospect it was clear from the start that she and Lorn had been strongly attracted to each other. She could picture him now, foot resting on the window seat as he had stared out at the lawns of Greenan Towers. Her breath had caught in her throat at the sheer masculine power of him. It still did. Surely she must have know that from the first he was as sexually aware of her as she was of him? Of course she did. So why hadn't she considered the implications? Why had she never stopped to think where all their lovemaking was leading? Lorn was a strong character, a passionate lover, there was no way their romance would begin and end with a few kisses.

'All or nothing,' he had said.

She bit her lip. Too late she wondered what Lorn would have expected of her as his wife. Perhaps he would have been happy for her to continue working? Perhaps they could have worked together, they made a good team. But suppose he was like Mike? There was a hard lump in her chest. Suppose he paid lip service to her ambitions until they were married, and then changed his mind the minute she was his? She had escaped Mike's cage by the skin of her teeth. Only a fool would rush into one of Lorn's construction. There would be no escape from that. Once they were man and wife she would be trapped.

Restlessly she rolled on to her back and stared at the ceiling. Silver and black shadows intermingled. But why must they be married? Wouldn't it be better for them to live together for a while? The idea wasn't so shocking. Plenty of couples, young and not-so-young, lived together on a trial basis, and usually wound up getting married once they were sure of their feelings. A breathing space would be wise. After all, she and Lorn had only known each other for a short time. It made sense not to rush things.

The more Zee considered the idea, the more she liked it. She started to smile, her heart lifting. As soon as she returned to London she would go and see Lorn, and this time she would *make* him listen to her point of view. This time she wouldn't allow him to silence her, and this time *he would accept her proposal*.

CHAPTER SEVEN

IT was early morning when her flight landed at Heathrow. It was raining and cold, and everything looked grey—grey skies, grey runway, grey people. Catching a glimpse of her reflection in the smoked glass walls of the corridor, Zee grimaced. She looked grey, too. Shadows around her eyes, limp hair, bedraggled jumpsuit, she looked like something the cat had brought home. But tomorrow.... Her head swam as she clutched at the handrail of the moving walkway. Tomorrow she would be rested. Tomorrow she would see Lorn.

Emotionally she rejected outright the notion that he might no longer be in London. He *had* to be here, he *had* to, she convinced herself, clenching her fists, willing it to be so. According to her calculations it was likely he had arrived back two days ago and would be reporting to Mr Edgar on his schemes for the Pantai Tropika Hotel. Although he showed little deference to his half-brother, business procedures needed to be followed, and Lorn was thoroughly conventional where business was concerned. As Zee waited at the baggage carousel, she decided that even if a fresh location was lined up for him, he would require a few days in which to assimilate the facts. He might resemble a human dynamo, but there was no way he could have flown across half the world and immediately embarked on another journey. She hoped....

Leaving the tube train at the Embankment, she checked into a small hotel near the river. The porter greeted her with delighted familiarity, for over the years she had often stayed there on her journeys to and from Malaysia. Picking at a late breakfast, she gave sleep the priority, and after two cups of tea and a dish of grapefruit segments, she went up to her room. Drawing thick curtains against the grey morning drizzle, she shed her clothes and nestled down in bed. Even the hum of vacuum cleaners farther along the corridor did not keep her from sleep.

It was late afternoon when she awoke. She felt great. Her plan had been to contact Lorn the following day, but she had only been out of bed two minutes before she was wildly rifling through her bag, tossing lipsticks and credit cards aside as she searched for his telephone number. What was the point of waiting? She felt fine now, invigorated after her sleep. The sooner she spoke to him, the sooner they would be together again. Flicking through the pages of her address book, she found Lorn's office telephone number. He had given it to her at Greenan Towers, instructing her to ring if she ever needed him. And now she did. . . .

Foolishly her fingers shook as she dialled. 'Could I speak to Mr Jensen?' she croaked, swallowing to ease a throat suddenly rough as sandpaper.

'Mr Jensen is presently away on business,' an officious female voice informed her.

Zee's heart sank. 'I need to speak to him.'

'He's due back tomorrow,' the woman said briskly. It would be Miss Canning, Zee decided. She had the clipped schoolmarm manner of a woman who had scant patience for the frailties and whims of the human race.

'What time tomorrow?'

'Early.'

'How early?' It was as though she was drawing blood.

Miss Canning gave an impatient click of her tongue. 'He's flying back from Glasgow on the first morning shuttle, but I doubt he'll be available in the office until the following day. I suggest you leave a message.'

'No. No, thank you,' said Zee, hurriedly replacing the receiver.

She was as nervous as a schoolgirl, and sat staring at the telephone for several minutes, quite desolate.

Gradually her natural optimism reasserted itself. She ran herself a hot bath, and as she lay in the scented water, she decided that as usual she had been too impulsive, but that, on this occasion, fate had played a wise card. Her original timing did make more sense. Although for the moment she was rested, experience warned her that jet lag would soon return and in an hour or two her energy would fade. Far better to take things at a reasonable pace and be properly refreshed by the morning. Reconciled to not seeing Lorn that day, Zee shampooed her hair and spent a leisurely time varnishing her nails and shaping her brows. She intended to be at her best when they met again tomorrow.

Despite the December chill, her hands were clammy. A host of butterflies were beating their wings in her breast as Zee resolutely tucked her brown leather clutch bag beneath her arm and strode along, high-heeled winter boots tap-tapping on the cobblestones. By rights Lorn must live in the next house on the left. Even though at present only clipped fir trees in tubs stood outside neat doorways, the mews was attractive. In summer it would be a riot of colour when window-boxes and hanging baskets overflowed with scarlet geraniums and trailing blue lobelia.

The wind curved a gleaming red wing of hair beneath her jawline, then tossed it free. Distractedly Zee smoothed it down, but in vain, for the wind tugged a second time. Yes, number thirty-nine—Lorn's home. For a heart-stopping moment she studied the nameplate, summoned up courage to ring the bell. Taking a deep breath, she stretched out a finger and stabbed. A resulting shrill sounded inside the house, but there was no other sound. Tapping an impatient toe, she waited, then pushed back her sleeve to examine her watch. Surely Lorn must have returned from Glasgow by now, it was almost noon. Again she rang the bell and waited, biting her lower lip. No sound from within. Then it hit

her. Of course!—he had called in at his office and
decided to remain there and work for the rest of the
day. Typical Lorn! Why come home and take things
easy when he could wear himself out studying reports
and sending telexes?

With a flicker of exasperation, Zee decided there was
only one course of action. She must retrace her steps to
the High Street and flag down a taxi. In less than half
an hour she would be at his office. Restlessly she shifted
from one foot to the other. She didn't want to meet him
against the background of his working life where he
would be brisk and businesslike. She had wanted to catch
him alone, in his own home. Spinning on her heel, she
faced the door. One last try. She was poised to prod her
finger at the bell again when she stiffened. There was a
moving shape behind the frosted panel, a tall white figure.

When Lorn opened the door he was still fumbling
with the tie belt of a terry towelling robe which reached
his knees. Bare legs and feet told her he was naked
beneath it.

'Hello,' he said, blinking stupidly. 'What time is it?'

No surprise. No kiss. No 'go away, I've nothing more
to say' or even 'how lovely to see you, my darling'.

'Er—five to twelve,' she got out.

'I feel like death warmed up.' He turned and
disappeared into the house before she had time to
realise much more than that he had obviously just got
out of bed, for his hair was rumpled and his eyes hardly
focusing. Lorn shambled off through a small hall,
leaving her no alternative but to follow.

With a click she closed the front door, and went after
him into a large living-room. For a moment he paused,
as though about to speak, but he thought better of it
and instead made for sliding glass doors at the far end
of the room. Zee looked around her. The living-room
was impressive, elegantly decorated in pale shades. The
walls were off-white, filled with batches of watercolours
and appliquéd pictures, while a thick creamy carpet
covered the floor. A white leather sofa, spilling with

rust and grey cushions, stood before a futuristic stainless steel grate, and at the windows were long cream curtains with a rust and grey motif. Splashes of rich colour were provided by flamboyant arrangements of flame and russet chrysanthemums in polished flagons. Part of her mind veered as she followed Lorn's tall silent figure, and she wondered who was responsible for the beautiful flower arrangements. Was some florist handsomely paid to keep his home regularly supplied or—her stomach twisted—had he brought Renate back to London with him? Her steps faltered across the shaggy pile. 'Are you here alone?' she asked the broad back.

He didn't turn. 'Yes.'

He was moving as though on automatic pilot. Sliding back the plate glass door, he crossed a compact dining area and made for the kitchen beyond a pine shelved room divider. Blindly he reached for a coffee percolator, fitting in the plug at the second try. He yawned. 'What are you doing here?' he asked, rubbing his eyes.

'I've come to see you.'

'Oh.' Lorn ran his hand across the rough stubble on his jaw, waiting.

Zee didn't know what to say next. 'I'm—I'm sorry if I got you out of bed,' she began.

'Don't be,' he interrupted. 'It's high time I was up. I've slept the clock round.' Wearily he raked the hair from his brow.

'But didn't you travel back from Glasgow this morning?'

He shook his head. 'I finished early and managed to catch a plane last night. I felt shattered and went straight to bed when I arrived home. I guess jet-lag is catching up on me.' He lifted two mugs from a cupboard and reached for the sugar. 'Just a quick coffee before you go,' he announced brusquely.

Zee's chin lifted. 'Who says I'm going?'

'I do. I don't entertain young ladies when I'm

virtually naked.' He tightened the belt of his robe. 'I know my limitations.'

'Don't you want to go back to bed?' she asked, raising a brow. 'With me?'

Lorn put his hands on the work surface behind him and leant back, examining her. 'Is that what you've come for? To proposition me?'

She flushed, feeling cheap and hating it. Inch by inch he was regaining consciousness, but inch by inch he was becoming more assertive, more aloof. A smooth coating of cold control was rolling over him.

'Lorn——' she pleaded, taking a step towards him, but he moved aside.

'Now it's my turn to yell don't touch me,' he said with a laugh that never reached his eyes.

Her lips compressed. Approaching him wasn't going to be easy. Suddenly her suggestion of them living together began to seem a trifle rash.

'I'll be back in a minute,' he said, breaking the silence, and swung away through a door which presumably led to his bedroom.

After a moment she heard the distant buzz of an electric razor. She ran a desultory finger along the work surface. The kitchen was in white and tobacco brown, equipped with all the latest labour-saving devices— washing machine, infra-red grill, dishwasher, small fridge and freezer. Lorn's home life seemed to be as immaculately organised as his business activities. Glossy pot plants vied with rows of bright paperbacks on the shelves of the pine partitioning. Everything was clean and neat.

Walking round to the dining area, Zee shrugged off her coat, laying it on a chair. She was beginning to feel as edgy as when she first met him. Unsuccessfully she looked around for a mirror and was forced to settle for a quick smoothing flick of fingers at her red hair. Pushing the sleeves of her pale green sweater up past her wrists, she returned to the kitchen. The surge of pale coffee rose and fell in the glass dome of the percolator. She sighed, fiddling nervously with the buttons on the fir green waistcoat which matched her corduroy skirt. If only Lorn wasn't so damned arrogant!

'I'm leaving for the office in half an hour,' he warned in a cool voice, coming back into the kitchen. He had washed and shaved, though the terry towelling robe was still unchanged. The transformation into Lorn Jensen, businessman, was halfway complete, and Zee's heart began to sink.

Calmly he poured two cups of coffee and added cream from the fridge. 'We'll have it in the lounge.' He gave a small concessionary smile and briefly the groove in his cheek flashed, giving her a measure of courage.

'Can we talk, Lorn?' she asked, sitting beside him on the sofa. She was trying to appear calm and casual, but inwardly there was a cauldron of bubbling emotions.

He shrugged. 'It depends what you want to talk about.'

His offhand manner grated. She didn't know where to start. He was waiting for her, long fingers tapping out a staccato rhythm on the broad leather arm of the sofa. She wondered why it sounded like machine-gun fire. Nervously she licked her lips with the tip of her tongue. 'Can we talk about marriage?'

A nerve leapt in his temple. *'No!'*

'Not on a personal basis,' she waffled, hot colour mounting in her cheeks. 'Just generally. You never told me what you expected from a wife, and I'd like to know.'

He shifted from her side to reach for his cup on the long low table before them. 'What the hell for?' he snorted.

As he moved the towelling robe gaped at his chest, giving Zee a tantalising glimpse of tanned skin and matted golden hair. She took a deep breath. 'We never did talk about your ideas for the future, did we? It was invariably me spouting *my* requirements. I wondered what you had in mind.'

'Oh yes?' A sardonic brow arched, sending icicles to pierce her heart. God, but he was making her squirm! Zee's thoughts flashed to the unknown Mr Edgar. How she pitied him, having to bear the brunt of Lorn's disdain as an ongoing thing, year in, year out. If only she could break through the brittle veneer to the loving man she knew existed within! She glanced at him beneath curling lashes. Lorn was leaning back, idly sipping his coffee, bare legs outstretched.

'Aren't your feet cold?' she asked irrationally.

The unexpected question startled him. 'No, they're always warm—feel them,' he replied without thinking.

Reaching down, she touched the arch of his foot. It was smooth, and firm, and warm. Instinctively she ran her fingertips across it, enjoying the sensation of skin on skin. 'You're right,' she said, twisting back her head to smile at him.

'Damn you!' he snapped angrily, clattering his cup and saucer down on the table.

Before she realised what was happening, he had dragged her hard against him, his mouth descending in a greedy bitter kiss which was over as abruptly as it had begun. Breathing raggedly, Lorn pushed himself from her and strode across the room to pick a worked silver box from an antique table. His back was towards her, the wide shoulders moving beneath the white towelling as he sought to control himself.

In bewilderment Zee touched her bruised lips with the back of her hand. 'I love you,' she said. At first there was no response and she shook her head in silent desperation. What did he want? She felt weak and shaky and disorientated by his embrace.

When he spoke, his voice was low. 'But not enough.'

He took a long time to light his cigarette, and when he turned back to face her he was icily in control, only the troubled expression in his eyes revealing any weakness.

'You're too hard, Lorn,' she flared, suddenly angry. 'Too hard on me, and too hard on yourself. Why must it always be take it or leave it? Why can't we discuss things? Why can't we compromise?'

His lip curled. 'Because I don't believe in compromise, that's why.' Inhaling deeply, he threw her a challenging sneer. 'And basically, neither do you, sweetheart. Do you?'

She opened her mouth to protest, but the look in his eyes silenced her.

'You were straight with me from the start, Zee, but I was too goddamn pigheaded to believe you when you maintained that your career came first. Foolishly I imagined I only had to say I loved you, and you'd come running.' Irritably he ground the half-smoked cigarette into an ashtray. 'I should have had more sense!'

Helplessly Zee moved her shoulders. 'But it needn't be the end, Lorn. Surely we can work something out?'

'I don't see how. I'd be perfectly happy for my wife to work for a year or two, but I *do* want children. And I want them while I'm young enough to enjoy them. I can't wait until you're thirty-five.' His mouth twisted. 'I want what I've never had—a proper family. I want a house in the country, kids, a dog, and a wife at the heart of it all, loving me and looking after us. And the older I get, the *more* I want it.'

'Maybe my ideas would change over the years. Thirty-five isn't a deadline. It could be much earlier.'

'And where the hell does that leave me?' he demanded, nostrils flaring. 'You have to commit yourself now, Zee.'

'Why?' She stood up to face him. 'Why now? Why must it be all cut and dried this instant? Why must I agree to exactly what *you* want, no questions asked?'

Frowning at her distraught face, he took a step towards her. 'I'm not asking you to walk into a cage so that I can slam the door and throw away the key! I want you to be my wife, my partner, not my bloody prisoner. Don't imagine I shall be like your father. I have no intention of dumping you in some situation you don't like, and leaving you to fend for yourself.' A half smile lifted the corner of his mouth. 'In any case, you're far too spirited not to play hell about it.'

Zee swallowed hard. Unconsciously her fingers balled into tight fists. 'I—I have a suggestion to make,' she said at last. 'Why don't we live together, say for six months or so, on a trial basis? It would give us time to get to know one another properly, and if all went well we could be married at the end of it.' She stared down at her boots. 'I might decide a house in the country is what I really want.'

'A trial run!' He looked at her in amazement. 'You want us to have a trial run! God! I ought to put you over my knee and beat the living daylights out of you,' he spat contemptuously. 'What the hell do you think I am? Some object you can take on a sale or return basis? Think again, sweetheart. Look what happened the last time you played that game—you left the poor devil flat in six weeks. Six bloody weeks!'

'That was different—Mike wasn't like you.'

'Like hell he wasn't,' Lorn cut in. 'Because there's no way I would live with you without a marriage certificate. Don't think I can't imagine what would happen. One day you'd forget to take the pill and you'd wind up pregnant. Then you'd concoct some hare-brained scheme and decide there was really no reason to get married. Without warning you'd move out, and my child would end up as a bastard, like his father.' His blue eyes glittered. 'No, thank you, not that. I wouldn't wish that on anyone.'

'But if I had a baby we'd be married,' she said, shocked at his suggestion.

'How do I know? You're a creature of impulse, Zee. I'm not taking you unless I know you're mine, really mine. You want me without any ties. How do I know it wouldn't be the same with my child?'

'It just wouldn't.'

The savagery of his words bowed her shoulders. What did he think she was, some selfish creature without one ounce of responsibility? She licked dry lips.

'Plenty of couples live together and most of them eventually get married.'

He glared at her. 'Well, it might work for them, but I know it wouldn't for me.' He stuck his hands into the pockets of his robe. 'I tried it once.'

'You never told me!'

'Why should I? It was years ago. It has nothing to do with you and me. The whole experience was a fiasco. We spent all our time discreetly pretending not to care too much. If either of us was late home, or went out alone for the evening the other one never dared ask questions in case they appeared to be too possessive. We fell over backwards trying not to pry—it was unreal. On one memorable occasion my plane was delayed overnight, and when I arrived back the next day the girl never even asked where I'd been. It was a relief when we broke up.'

Zee sighed. 'But it wouldn't be like that with us—we love each other.'

'Yes,' he said heavily, 'I believe we do, but I need security, Zee. I can't live on a knife edge. I'm sorry, but I can't.'

She made an exasperated gesture. 'But even marriage isn't one hundred per cent cast-iron certain. The divorce rate gets higher each year.'

'I know that, but at least if you are married you have made a firm promise, and most people get married intending it to last. You would, wouldn't you?' She nodded. 'Marriage gives you room for manoeuvre. Sure, you have rows as you adjust to living together, but you also work damned hard to resolve them. You would think twice about walking out.' Lorn rubbed the back of his neck with long fingers. 'If you'd been married to Mike you wouldn't have left him after six weeks, would you?'

'No, but. . . .'

He held up a silencing hand. 'There you are. You would have tried damned hard to make a succees of it.'

'It was all wrong between Mike and me,' she said

flatly. 'Wrong! It would have been just as wrong if we'd been married.' Her lips tightened. 'No doubt we would have stayed together longer, years perhaps, but they would have been miserable years, and perhaps we would have had children and they would have been involved. Any marriage between Mike and me would have been destined to come to an end eventually.'

'But you never gave it a chance,' he insisted. 'If you'd stayed around you might have discovered a formula that suited you both. Instead, the first time he forgot to dry the dishes, off you dashed!'

'That's not true! The domestic side wasn't really an issue—it was just that. . . .' She could feel her temperature rising. 'Well—er—physically he didn't turn me on.' She dropped her head, studying her boots again.

Lorn grunted. 'Come off it, Zee. You're a passionate woman, you enjoy lovemaking.'

'With you, Lorn,' she gulped. 'But not with Mike.'

'You can't expect me to believe that!'

'Why not?' she cried.

His eyes flicked scornfully over her. 'The crux of the matter, sweetheart, is that you aren't ready for marriage and I refuse to live in sin. So I guess we're back to square one.' He examined his wristwatch. 'And now, if you'll excuse me, I must get dressed. Perhaps you'll show yourself out.' He started to move away towards the bedroom. It was dismissal.

'You bastard!' she spat out before she could stop herself.

He folded his arms. 'And we're back to *that* too, are we?'

'No!' Zee's hand flew to her throat in agitation. 'I didn't mean it like that.'

There was a reluctant murmur of agreement. 'I know,' he said, suddenly gentle, a nerve twitching in his cheek.

Her eyes swam with unshed tears. 'I don't care that you're illegitimate. That was nothing at all to do with my feelings on marriage.'

'I know that too, and thank you.'

She brushed past him, collecting her coat and dragging it on as she made for the front door.

In silence Lorn followed her. 'Do you want a job with the Devenay hotels when you finish in Scotland?' he asked, pulling back the catch.

Zee stomped out on to the step. 'No, thank you.'

'Why not?'

Unable to meet his eyes, she took a long time putting on her gloves. 'Because I don't want you pulling strings on my behalf,' she said at last.

He ignored her tart tone. 'I wouldn't. You sure know me better than that. I don't employ deadwood. You're an intelligent woman, full of fresh ideas. You'd be an asset.'

'No, thank you,' she repeated firmly.

'Are you travelling back to Scotland today?' he asked, not wanting to let her go, and despising himself for the feeling.

'I suppose so.' If the truth was told, she hadn't planned that far.

'Take care.'

'Yes.' She pulled at her gloves again. 'Are you going to visit Greenan Towers again, or has your henchman taken charge?'

'Do you want me to come?' he asked quietly, lounging against the door frame, hands in his pockets.

Zee raised her head, defiantly meeting his eyes. 'No, no,' she cried rashly. 'No, don't come. I never want to see you again!'

'Right then, sweetheart, you never will.' He stood up straight, turning away before she could see the pain in his eyes.

CHAPTER EIGHT

ZEE buried her head in the bouquet of dark red roses, breathing deeply. Mmm, the fragrance from the velvety blooms was sweet. A young man, sitting on the far side of the waiting room, grinned at her delight, and she gave a tremor of a smile before sliding her eyes from him. A new father, she decided, noting the bottle of cordial and bulging plastic carrier clutched in his hands. She checked her watch against the large round clock on the wall. Only a few minutes to wait now. The room was crowded, all the chairs had been taken long ago, and people were standing in groups or waiting outside in the corridor. As the minutes ticked by, the air of expectancy mounted. She knew that the moment the Sister appeared, there would be one almighty rush for the maternity ward.

Her mind retreated to the first time she had been at the hospital. She and Struan had been as jumpy as cats on a hot tin roof as they waited to visit Carol. Struan had been present at Emma's birth, but six hours later, when they had arrived for the daily visiting hour, he was still high on happiness, hardly making any sense at all.

Looking back, they all seemed so young. At the time Zee had been convinced Carol was heading for disaster, saddling herself with a baby when she was barely twenty, and less than a year after her marriage. Now Zee conceded that life was working out well for her sister. Since Zee's return to Scotland, Carol had been on a far more even keel now that the early morning sickness was abating. She was beginning to bloom. Once the first torturous months were over, Carol always flourished, her hair taking on an extra sheen, her skin becoming peachy-smooth. Zee knew

Carol was destined to become disgustingly serene and contented.

'Time to go in now, ladies and gentlemen,' a brisk voice announced from the doorway and, as expected, the room emptied in seconds.

Zee allowed herself to be steered along in the surge, and it was only when she had passed through wide doors at the entrance to the ward that she was given time to pause. Neat beds with bright floral covers to match the curtains were arranged down both sides of the long room, tiny cribs in pink and blue stationed at the foot of each. Already admiring mums were showing their offspring to equally admiring dads, and grandmothers and grandfathers. There was a great deal of gushing and cooing. The wave of a hand halfway down the ward attracted her attention, and she strode forward.

'Many congratulations, Heather,' she smiled, handing over the roses. She kissed the girl's cheek. 'Aren't you clever!'

'Yes, I am,' Heather agreed, with a vast smug smile. 'Have a peep at him. Isn't he a lovely wee bairn? He's the very image of Duggie.'

Zee leaned over the crib. The baby was so small, tiny dark head, a flailing fist searching for the rosebud mouth.

'He's beautiful,' she said, and her voice cracked. Her eyes were damp. Several times she blinked, but even so she could hardly see for the blur of tears. Taking out her handkerchief, she blew her nose.

'Everyone has been very kind,' Heather said encouragingly, giving Zee time to compose herself. 'Mr McCrimmon and his wife sent me a beautiful cot blanket, and Aileen and Gary brought a baby bath.'

Zee swallowed hard. There was a lump in her throat which refused to go down. She nodded, unable to speak. Again she looked at the boy child. Lorn had been like that once, she thought. So innocent, so in need of love and protection, and, like Heather's baby, without his natural birthright, without a father he could call his own. She twisted her handkerchief in her fingers.

'Have—have you heard from Duggie?'

'He's been once but—well, it's rather awkward.' Heather traced a pattern on the bedspread. 'It'll be easier when we're home.'

'Yes.'

'Didn't I time it well?' she demanded, with a bright smile. 'I held on until you came back from Malaysia before I gave birth.'

Zee was able to speak now. 'You certainly did,' she agreed. And you allowed me a week to settle in too, before disappearing. *And* it was on a Sunday, not even in working hours!'

Heather laughed. 'I'll be back on the first of February for definite. Have you started looking for another job?'

'I've been scanning the newspapers and trade journals,' Zee confessed, tucking her handkerchief away in her bag. 'But I've not applied for anything yet. As Greenan Towers is to be closed throughout January, I finish there at the end of December. After Hogmanay I shall go and stay with a girl friend in London. It's more convenient to be based down there when I have interviews to attend.'

'Did you know Mr McCrimmon was considering leaving the hotel?' Heather asked.

Zee's brows shot to her hairline.

'When he and his wife came to visit me, it slipped out that his brother has bought a tea-room in Oban. Apparently he's pushing Mr McCrimmon to go into partnership, and he's very tempted.'

Heather chatted on about this and that, but Zee's attention was far away. Mr McCrimmon had said nothing to her about leaving. She wondered what Lorn's role was in this unexpected turn of events. Had he bluntly told the manager to go? It would be in character. She knew he considered the man a loafer, and he would have no compunction about getting rid of him, even if Mr Edgar felt otherwise. Doubtless the mention of the Oban tea-shop was an excuse to cover the real reason for the departure. Mr McCrimmon was merely saving face.

She caught her full lower lip between her teeth. Her contact with Lorn, since coming back to Scotland, had been virtually nil, although he was in daily contact with Miles Lang, the young consultant who was now supervising the alterations. Only once had Zee spoken to him, and that had been purely by chance. Heather had been gossiping with Mrs Weir in the kitchen when a London call had come through the switchboard.

'Good morning, Greenan Towers. Can I help you?' Zee has asked brightly.

'My God, but you're efficient,' a cool voice had mocked.

'Lorn!'

'I want to speak to Miles Lang,' he had demanded, making her wonder if the trace of humour had been imaginary. Flicking the necessary switches with trembling fingers, she had put him through without another word. Even if her throat hadn't suddenly been paralysed with longing, she wouldn't have known what to say. Since then it had always been Miss Canning who had come on to the line before Lorn was linked with Miles. She didn't know if he was deliberately using his secretary as a buffer, but it looked that way.

The shrill of an electric bell rang around the ward, ripping into her thoughts.

'My word, doesn't time fly?' Heather declared. 'Before you go, would you pass my wee laddie to me, Zee? It's nearly feeding time.'

Zee was all sixes and sevens as she lifted the baby. At nine months, Gordie seemed huge in comparison, she had forgotten how tiny newborn babies were. At last the thumb had located the rosebud mouth and he was sucking away, tiny starfish hand covering most of his face.

'He's lovely,' she said breathlessly, thrusting him into his mother's arms and turning away, her eyes bright again with tears.

She was grateful the bus was almost empty. After noisily blowing her nose a few times, she devoted her attention to the view, enjoying the clean rolling lines of the Ayrshire hills. The winter countryside was bare, whipped watercolour pale by the December wind. Long ago leaves had been shed, and now the branches of the trees were silhouetted like stiff lace against the sky. She wondered why Heather's baby had upset her so much. Although she had seen both Emma and Gordie when they were newly born, they hadn't touched her heart in this way. Zee frowned at the grey slant of the distant sea. Surely she wasn't becoming broody? Surely she wasn't going to turn into another softhearted woman, cooing over prams and babies in the park? Tossing her head, she stifled the idea. Be sensible, she told herself. Imagine the satisfaction you'll derive from a career. Any fool can produce a baby, but it takes drive and dedication to become a top-flight woman executive. Think how everyone will envy your independent lifestyle and expensive clothes. . . .

Lamps, glowing out like welcoming beacons, were already lit when she returned to Greenan Towers. With the shortest day imminent, daylight faded mid-afternoon and although it was not much after four o'clock, already it was dusk. Zee eased open the top button of her coat as she crossed to the reception counter. Miles Lang was installed behind it, his sandy-coloured hair flopping over his brow as he studied the pile of papers before him.

'Hello, dear girl,' he smiled, looking up. 'I didn't expect you to come back here today. I thought you'd go straight home.'

Zee lifted the hinged top of the counter and joined him.

'I do work until five,' she told him jauntily, 'and it's

not fair to take off more time than is necessary. It was decent of Mr McCrimmon to allow me to visit Heather, and of you to step in here. I appreciate it.'

Stretching, he rose to his feet. 'No sweat. It's been pretty quiet. Hardly anyone's been or gone all afternoon, so I've enjoyed playing receptionist with only the phone to deal with.'

'We only have two commercial travellers staying here at present,' she said, slinging her coat on to the back of her chair. 'I dare say they'll be back later for dinner.'

Miles eyed her up and down, appreciating the curves beneath her emerald green jersey dress. 'I'm enjoying the change from the London scene. The office is always highly charged. It's impossible to take things easy if Lorn is around. By the way, he rang.'

'Oh yes,' she said, sitting down quickly.

'He wanted the usual progress report. He's told me to prod the decorators if they don't look like finishing the bedrooms by the end of the week.' Miles sighed. 'He doesn't seem to realise it'll soon be Christmas and everything is beginning to slacken off.'

'Are you going to London for the holiday?' she asked.

His boyish face lit up. 'Yes, back home to Mum and Dad and all the relatives. We always have a real family Christmas. It's great!'

Pressing her lips tightly together, Zee wished there wasn't going to be a Christmas this year, though she supposed she was fortunate to be spending it with Carol and Struan. At least she wouldn't be alone. Perhaps she was destined to spend all her future Christmases with them. After all, the festive time *was* for families, as Miles had said. She had a horrifying vision of herself as the maiden aunt, trotting up to Scotland each year, bearing gaily wrapped parcels for Carol's brood of children. She wondered if Lorn would be travelling to Denmark to spend the holiday with his mother. Perhaps not. It would be more in character for him to devote the entire period to work.

'By the way,' Miles continued, 'Lorn said to tell you there's a fantastic job going with the Americana line. He says they're advertising today in the *Telegraph*.'

'Thanks,' she muttered. 'I'll have a look when I get home.'

Struan had already spotted the advertisement, and the newspaper was propped up on the sideboard, folded at the right page, black Biro circling the details.

'Sounds great, doesn't it?' he demanded, sitting impatiently on the arm of the settee as she scanned the information. 'Tailor-made—you have all the qualifications they require. It's a cinch!'

'Some hopes,' she retaliated, but the advertisement did sound promising. The worldwide hotel group required a young person with sound management background, to take up a post, initially as personal assistant to the Chief Executive.

'Excellent career prospects, it says. You'll be on the board before you know it,' he teased, looking over her shoulder. His face became serious. 'I mean it, Zee. They're a young go-ahead group, with a fine reputation. There's plenty of opportunity for travel, which is what you want.' He pointed to the advertisement. 'The first three months based at the New York headquarters, and after that the suitable applicant would be expected to be free to travel internationally.'

'That's you,' said Carol, coming into the room. 'Married men wouldn't want to be continually on the move. I reckon a determined career woman, with no ties, is exactly what they're looking for.'

Struan nudged Zee. 'If I was the Chief Executive, I'd much rather have a sexy redhead travelling with me than some sombre-suited businessman!'

'Sexist!' Carol laughed, flopping down in a chair. She pushed the hair from her eyes. 'Thank goodness both the kids are fed and watered. With luck we should have another quiet night. Gordie's teething troubles seem to have stopped.'

'For the time being,' her husband commented drily.

She ignored him. 'What does Heather's baby look like?' she asked Zee, leaning forward.

'He's lovely, so small and delicate. When I held him in my arms I felt quite overwhelmed.'

'How much does he weigh?'

'He was seven pounds when he was born, but already he's put on two ounces.'

'Here we go again,' said Struan with a noisy sigh. 'Undiluted baby talk for the next hour solid!' He folded his arms and grinned. 'I'm surprised at you, Zee. I thought career-orientated ladies preferred to discuss the state of the stock market, rather than birthweights!'

Zee stuck out her tongue.

'So do you intend to apply?' Carol asked, nodding towards the paper.

'I—I don't know. I'll think it over for a few days.'

'Why waste time?' her sister persisted. 'Write tonight. Get your application in first—show them that you're keen.'

Zee wrinkled her nose. 'There's no rush. I'm just not sure if I fancy all the travelling. It sounds exciting, but in reality it could be rather lonely.'

'But it's what you've always wanted,' Carol declared. 'Well, at least since Mike left the scene.'

'And what do you mean by that?' Zee demanded, flicking back her hair. 'I've always been ambitious, even before Mike.'

'What she means is that you weren't such a dedicated career woman,' Struan intervened peaceably. 'It's only since he hurt you that you've become obsessed with your work.'

'He *didn't* hurt me!'

Struan gazed around the room, as though seeking assistance from an invisible source. 'Okay, so *you* walked out on him, but the fact remains that you suffered. I know you, Zee, and I'd bet even money you rushed him into that flat on the spur of the moment, and then wished like hell you hadn't been so impulsive.'

She shifted uneasily. 'Maybe I did. It was all a big mistake, but I'm over it now.'

There was a pregnant pause.

'Is Lorn coming up to Scotland before Christmas?' Carol asked offhandedly.

Zee gritted her teeth. She wasn't fooled by the innocent query. She had given her sister only a sketchy outline of what had happened abroad, but she knew Carol hoped for a reconciliation. It had been too embarrassing to tell Carol about her visit to his home. Her heart beat a little faster when she thought of her suggestion to him that they live together. Now it seemed like an insult. She wondered how she could ever have imagined the idea would appeal to a proud man like Lorn, with his background.

'No,' she said flatly. She had no idea of his plans, but as he had told her they would never meet again, she presumed he would keep well away from Greenan Towers until she had gone. Her stomach plunged. *Lorn* had asked Miles to tell her about the advertisement, so he must have read it and be well aware that the post was initially based in New York, and then involved worldwide travel. Now it was sickeningly clear. Lorn had accepted the fact that she had no further place in his life, and was indifferent to the knowledge that in future they could be oceans apart.

She struggled to her feet. 'I—I think that was Gordie crying,' she lied breathlessly. 'I'll go and check.'

On winged feet she sped from the room and up the stairs. It was only when she collapsed on her bed that the tight control cracked, and the tears came. 'Lorn, I love you,' she sobbed into the pillow. 'I want you. I want to marry you!'

CHAPTER NINE

A TALL fir tree in a wooden tub stood halfway down the lobby, filling the wide angle of the staircase. Already well bedecked, its thick-needled boughs were bending with the weight of bright baubles and multi-coloured lights.

'Spend your Christmas at Greenan Towers, and we'll make it a Christmas to remember,' Miles boomed with mock pomposity from the foot of the ladder. He grinned up at Zee, perched on the topmost step, as she stretched to fix a bewinged fairy to the peak of the tree.

'Hey, suppose we suggest to Lorn that we advertise the hotel on television? We could compose a jingle and sing it together. We'd kit you out in a Santa Claus outfit, with a very short skirt.' He leered up at her. 'Mind you, the view from here's not half bad.'

'*Miles!*'

'It's vital I keep control of the stepladder down here, while you're precariously involved with the artistic matters up there,' he justified, frankly admiring her stance. 'It's just that I've never seen legs so long before.'

'Well, look the other way,' she laughed. 'I knew I should have worn trousers this morning.'

'It isn't the Devenay tradition for Devenay female staff to dress in such casual attire,' he boomed again.

'No sir.' She gave a grinning salute as she shifted her position to a more discreet angle. Zee cut an attractive figure, warmly clad as she was in an oyster and bitter chocolate brown striped sweatshirt, teamed with brown skirt and knee-high suede boots.

Miles lolled against the stepladder. 'Let's crack open a bottle of champagne when you've finished decorating the tree,' he suggested. 'It's only three days to Christmas. It's time we got into the spirit of the thing.'

Zee reached down for a streamer of shimmering tinsel. 'You're in the spirit already,' she teased, twisting it amongst the dark green foliage. All morning the young man had been in a flippant mood, demob-happy, raring to get home. 'What time's your plane in the morning?'

He glanced round. 'It's this afternoon,' he said, lowering his voice. 'Don't tell a soul, but I'm sneaking off after lunch to catch the shuttle. I can't see any point in hanging around here. The workmen are trailing off. They're only doing dribs and drabs. Incidentally, if Lorn should ring, would you be a dear girl and lie through your teeth? Pretend I'm out chasing up the new curtains. What he doesn't know can't harm him.'

She pinned a scarlet metallic ball to the end of a branch. 'Is he expected to phone?' she asked, telling herself to keep her voice level. 'I understand he was away from the office.'

'He is, but he's a cunning character. He likes to keep tabs on the various projects, no matter where he is. It wouldn't surprise me if he telephoned Mr McCrimmon on Christmas Day!'

'I don't know why Greenan Towers is remaining open over Christmas,' she complained, taking a last bauble from the box.

'Profit, it's called,' he replied pithily. 'I understand Mr Edgar was all for closing down, but Lorn thought the dining-room would bring in a worthwhile return.'

'He's probably right.' Zee leant back to survey the tree. It sparkled with iridescent decorations in silver and gold, scarlet and green, and she gave a smile of satisfaction. Despite her original lack of enthusiasm for this year's festivities, a certain element of excitement was, nevertheless, beginning to flicker inside her.

'Terrific,' said Miles, rising to his feet and grinning at her. 'The tree's not bad, either.'

Gingerly Zee started to negotiate the steps. They were widely spaced, and in her tight skirt it was difficult to go down without revealing acres of thigh.

'I reckon your legs go right the way up to your shoulders,' Miles teased, enjoying her progress. 'You'll look a knockout in that Santa mini-skirt.' He paused. 'Or perhaps you could wear tinsel hot pants, or even a fur bikini.'

She started to laugh, and as she reached the second last step he put his hands around her waist to steady her.

'Okay, Lang, quit feeling up the hired help,' a deep voice rasped from the front door.

Swivelling in surprise, Zee almost fell off the ladder, and Miles' hands tightened to support her. Lorn was watching them. Judging by his tousled blond hair and the colour in his cheeks, he had recently walked in from the cold. Car keys dangled in his fingers, and Zee realised she and Miles must have been too engrossed to hear the arriving roar of the Porsche. She wondered how long he had been there.

'There goes my shuttle!' Miles whispered into her ear.

For a moment Lorn paused, frowning at the secretive aside, but he made no comment. Casually he smoothed down his windtossed tie, tucking it into his jacket, and turned to a man beside him.

'Edgar, I don't believe you've met Miles Lang. He's a hard worker when he isn't being enticed away by young ladies who should know better.'

'I'm not enticing him,' Zee protested, stepping down on to the wooden floor.

Her face flamed with colour as he patently overlooked her outburst. 'And this is Miss Robertson, so-called receptionist,' he drawled.

She opened her mouth to vindicate herself, but Mr Edgar was striding forward, hand outstretched, and she was forced to turn her attention to him.

'Good morning, so pleased to meet you,' he said.

Zee mustered up a polite response to his greeting. He seemed a friendly enough man, shorter and thicker-set than Lorn, and goodlooking in a fleshy sort of way. She decided she could detect a passing likeness, but whereas

Mr Edgar's face was soft and set into a pleasing smile, Lorn's was hard, blue eyes like ice pools in a bleak landscape.

'Would you care for a coffee?' Miles asked.

'No,' Lorn snapped.

'Yes, please,' his half-brother replied at the same moment.

Shrugging wide shoulders, Lorn gave way graciously. 'Okay, Miles, you take Edgar to meet Mr McCrimmon, will you? You can all have a coffee. While you're doing that Miss Robertson can show me what progress had been made with the new decorations.' He waited as Miles directed Mr Edgar towards the office, then said calmly, 'Lead the way.'

Somehow Zee marched ahead of him up the stairs, ignoring the eyes burning into her spine. 'The bedroom decorations are complete,' she said briskly, reaching the landing. 'The painters are doing bits and pieces in the lounge and dining-room, but they finish tomorrow. They'll be back to start on the bulk of the work a day or two after Hogmanay.'

'I'd forgotten everyone shuts up shop in Scotland for a couple of weeks over Christmas and New Year,' he commented drily.

It was nerve-racking, trying to appear cool and indifferent, when all the time her heart was beating like a jungle drum and her knees seemed in great danger of buckling. Turning into the corridor, she slung wide the first door. 'There you are.' Her nervousness was rapidly turning to anger, and suddenly it was all she could do to remain civil. How dared he arrive here out of the blue, and play havoc with her senses? It had taken painful days for her to assemble a porcelain-fine coating of emotional control, and now he was cracking through it, without effort. And how dared he imply that she and Miles had been misbehaving!

As he swept past her into the room, there was a tangy whiff of his aftershave to remind her of the intoxicating fragrance of his skin. She remembered his skin, soft and warm from the tropical sun. . . .

Standing in the centre of the room, Lorn gazed critically around. If he finds fault I'll murder him, she thought. He inspected the glossy woodwork, ran a finger down the wallpaper joints. Zee held her breath.

'Very nice,' he said at last.

'Of course the curtains are to be replaced. We've only re-hung the old ones for the time being, so that the windows don't look too desolate from the outside.' She gestured towards the twin beds. 'And new covers arrive early January.'

Lorn rested one hand on a low chest of drawers and thrust the other into his trouser pocket. Unwittingly her eyes followed his movement, drinking in the hard line of his thigh beneath the soft grey wool.

'Close the door,' he ordered. 'And lock it.'

'Lorn?' she queried, staring at him in bewilderment at this unexpected command.

Impatient with her lack of response, he strode to the door himself and shot the bolt. When he turned back to face her, his chest was rising and falling in agitation. For a tense moment their eyes collided, then Lorn spun away, striding abruptly to the window.

'What goes on between you and Miles Lang?' he demanded, folding his arms and glaring out blankly.

'No—nothing. He was helping me decorate the tree.'

'And getting a damn good look at your legs,' he said scathingly.

'What's wrong with that?' she demanded.

Swivelling, he confronted her. 'Nothing,' he growled, 'if it stops there, but does it?'

'Of course it does, he's only a boy,' Zee snapped, her temper galloping away. 'In any case, why do you care?'

'I haven't the slightest idea why,' he retorted coldly, 'but I do, and it's tearing me apart. God! Zee, I don't know right from wrong any more! I must be out of my mind, falling for a girl like you!'

Her eyes flashed green fire at the implied insult. 'What do you mean, a girl like me?'

'A girl who refuses marriage, but who wants to live with me like some—some. . . .' He lifted his hands in a helpless gesture and dropped them again.

'But you lived with a girl before.'

'I told you, that was different,' he said curtly. 'She was a self-possessed character. She'd been around. There was no danger of her acting rashly, foolishly. In no way was *she* vulnerable.'

'And *I* am?'

'Yes, you damn well are. I doubt you could function properly in a half-and-half situation, and that's what living together is,' he scolded. 'You've not thought it through properly, have you? The girl I lived with before had the whole scene taped in advance. She knew exactly how far she was prepared to go emotionally. She was methodical and level-headed.'

'She sounds like you,' Zee retorted.

'Like I *thought* I was,' he replied heavily, 'but now. . . .' He glowered at her. 'I always promised myself that when I found the right girl I would marry her straight away. Everything would be right and proper, but then—then you come along and want us to have an affair!' He uttered an oath.

Zee hung her head. 'I was wrong.'

'Wrong?' he echoed in disbelief.

'Wrong,' she repeated, and continued hurriedly, 'I was too impulsive, and I'm sorry. It was a foolish suggestion, I realise that now. I've changed my mind.'

Lorn's jaw clamped into steel. 'Changed your mind?' he sneered. 'Like you changed your mind over Mike? You mean—you mean you don't want us to live together?'

She shook her head slowly, polished red hair moving like the swell of a heavy sea. 'No, not now.'

Lorn swore again, very loudly and very crudely. 'It appears to me that there's only one wavelength on which we're destined to be in tune, sweetheart.' He stepped towards her, gripping her shoulders.

'Meaning?' Zee asked wildly.

'Meaning sex, and meaning that I damn well owe it to myself to make love to you at least once before you disappear.' His fingers were working compulsively into her flesh, massaging the skin beneath the velour sweatshirt.

'Disappear?' she echoed faintly, hypnotised by the seductive curve of his mouth, the rough golden hair on his upper lip.

As he bent his head to kiss her, he offered no explanation. Zee had no defence, nor wanted any. As Lorn's mouth covered hers, warm and moistly avid, her head swam, and willingly she offered herself to his passionate invasion. His hands tightened on her shoulders, pulling her against him, the hard male lines of his thighs telling her all she wanted to know—that he desired her. His jacket was unbuttoned, and she slipped her hands beneath it, spreading her fingers across his chest, absorbing the fiery heat of his body beneath the thin poplin. His hands slid down her back to her hips, dragging her to him with possessive pressure.

'I want you,' he said angrily, kissing her neck with a half-open mouth. She could feel the soft bite of his teeth on her skin; he was branding her as his own.

'You've turned my values upside down,' he muttered. 'All I care about now is making love to you, and to hell with the consequences.'

Wordlessly she stroked the fall of blond hair from his brow.

He was trembling. 'Please, Zee,' he begged in anguish. 'Now. Just once!'

'No, Lorn,' she said softly.

With an agonised groan he turned from her, leaning against the wall, his head buried against his arm as he summoned the discipline he needed. He took a deep breath. 'You're right.' In a daze he looked around, though he seemed scarcely to recognise his surroundings.

'We'd better go downstairs,' said Zee, loving him and

wanting him so much. So very much. 'The others will be wondering where we've disappeared to.'

With a sigh of frustration Lorn fastened his jacket. 'I'm sorry,' he said, shaking his head stupidly. 'I don't know what came. . . .'

As he opened the door there was the sound of footsteps on the stairs. Mr Edgar, Mr McCrimmon and Miles were turning on to the corridor. Straightening his tie with fingers now steady, Lorn walked forward to meet them. 'Everything is fine,' he announced decisively. 'Come and have a look, Edgar.'

As the men went on a tour of inspection, Zee returned to the reception desk. She didn't remember much of what she did for the rest of the morning. The accounts she was supposedly cross-checking made no sense, as her eyes skidded over the figures and her thoughts leapt away. Even when the switchboard shrilled it was an effort to answer coherently. All she could think about was Lorn. Lorn here. Lorn now. But when he led the men down the staircase and across the lobby into the office, he seemed hardly to notice her, his expression remote and businesslike. He had resumed control, of the situation and of himself.

Head buzzing, she stared at the same invoice for what seemed to be the twenty-third time. *Why* had he returned? Was it merely a business trip that he couldn't avoid? A sigh of regret acknowledged that he didn't appear to have come to offer her a second chance. He wasn't about to beg her to marry him. He had spoken of making love to her *once*. That certainly didn't sound as though he intended to do more than satiate his desire and drive promptly out of her life. She unwillingly recognised that it was probably only jealousy over Miles which had fanned his desire to white-hot proportions, where he had hardly known what he was doing. Lorn was too self-disciplined to allow such an occurrence to happen twice. Zee's stomach twisted. No doubt he was already regretting his impulsive desire to make love to her. Now that he was briskly in control again he would dismiss his earlier feelings for what they were, an impetuous emotional response.

The men were incommunicado until lunchtime, discussing the future of the hotel, and after a snack meal the talking continued. It was mid-afternoon when the office door opened and Miles emerged. He tiptoed over to Zee at the reception counter. 'Guess what!' he whispered, keeping one careful eye on the door behind him. 'I'm flying home today, as planned.'

She raised her brows in pleased collusion at his news. 'Did you ask permission?'

'Didn't have to. It turned out that Mr Edgar is taking the late afternoon shuttle to London, and Lorn suggested I join him.' He grinned gleefully. 'Lorn will drive us to Glasgow Airport in half an hour. I'm just off upstairs to collect my gear.'

Zee straightened the wad of papers on her desk. 'Is— is he coming back to Greenan Towers when he's dropped you off?' she asked jerkily.

'No. He's finished here. He's going to motor back to Birmingham, he's booked in at a Devenay hotel there tonight. In the morning he'll do the last lap down to London.'

Plagued with unhappy thoughts, Zee turned away to concentrate on the invoices. And later, when Lorn swooped across the lobby Miles and Mr Edgar in tow, his halfhearted gesture of farewell only confirmed her misery. Now she knew for certain that his lovemaking had been an aberration, and was not to be repeated. The afternoon dragged. All she wanted to do was find a dark corner and curl up. Part of her mind registered that snowflakes had begun to fall, but even so she was surprised when five o'clock came, and she emerged into the chill December night to discover the courtyard thickly white. There was a satisfying crunch beneath her boots as she strode towards the road. Tugging her coat collar around her ears, Zee thrust gloved hands deep into her pockets, and when a snowflake landed on the warm fullness of her lips she snaked out the tip of her tongue to absorb the icy morsel.

By the time she reached the bus stop her coat was crusted with snow. She frowned up into the glow of the street light. Snow was coming down thick and heavy, fat white flakes stark against the ebony sky. If it continued at this rate, the fall would be inches deep by morning. Her mind travelled to Lorn. He would be driving across the border from Scotland to England in an hour or two, and the Border hills were particularly prone to heavy snowfalls and drifting. He drove the Porsche expertly, but bad weather didn't differentiate. Expensive cars were as vulnerable to bad road conditions as lesser vehicles. Lips thinning, Zee decided her sympathy was misplaced. It would serve him right if he was trapped in the snow. He had caused her enough pain by suddenly reappearing again, it would be justice if his Scottish journey afforded him some discomfort too.

The bus was long overdue. Zee stamped her feet against the cold, wondering how long she would have to wait. Would it be better to walk? Ruefully she eyed the slender heels of her fashion boots. The pavements were already slippery with snow. There was no rush, although she was babysitting this evening Carol and Struan were not due out until after seven. Struan's employers were holding their annual Christmas dinner dance. The evening was the highlight of Carol's social calendar, and there had already been great excitement when she bought a new long evening dress, and splashed out on a pair of diamanté sandals.

Eventually the bus did arrive, and Zee boarded it with relief. Carol was almost ready when she reached the house, face carefully made up, hair shampooed and blow-dried into a shining cap.

'The children are already bathed,' she announced, cheeks pink. 'They're playing with their toys. I'll pop them into bed before we leave.' She led the way into the kitchen. 'Your dinner's in the oven, so while you're eating I'll get changed. Struan will be home soon.'

As Zee ate her solitary meal, she listened to the cacophony with an amused smile. The television was blaring from the lounge where Emma and Gordie cavorted on the rug with never a glance at the screen, while from upstairs came the sound of her sister, frantically rushing to and fro between bedroom and bathroom as she beautified herself. When Struan arrived the pace increased, and there were even more hurried comings and goings.

'You'd think you were preparing to meet Royalty,' Zee teased as her sister pirouetted before her. The children had been unceremoniously deposited in bed, and now it was seven o'clock.

'I intend to make a good impression on Struan's boss,' Carol protested.

'You will. One look at that cleavage and Struan'll be given instant promotion!'

Carol screwed up her nose and laughed. 'You can't really tell I'm pregnant yet, can you? Apart from the burgeoning bosom?'

'No. You look fantastic, all that glossy hair and glowing complexion. You'll be the prettiest one there. There's no sign of a bump,' Zee continued assuringly, as Carol glanced down at her white dress.

'Not yet, but just you wait!' Struan teased, coming into the room.

'It's Omar Sharif!' Zee gasped, staggering back on to the settee in mock horror. 'What happened to that crummy guy who digs the garden in baggy jeans and an elbowless sweater?'

Struan adjusted the cuffs of his frilly shirt beneath the smart dinner jacket and preened. 'Don't be jealous because you can't come to the ball, Cinders.' He gave her a wink. 'Do hurry up, Carol. I'll be turning back into a frog or something if we don't leave soon!'

When they had gone the house was quiet—too quiet. There was suddenly too much time to think, and too many things to think about. Zee switched on the television, but after staring at it blankly for an hour, switched it off again. In a desultory fashion she skipped through the pages of the daily newspaper, and scanned some magazines. At nine o'clock she bathed, then wandered downstairs again. It was too early to go to bed; she knew she would never sleep. There was no sound from the children. Pulling her velour dressing-gown around her, she sat on the settee and re-varnished her nails, long legs tucked beneath her.

It was a quiet night, the snow still falling softly, muffling the sounds of the world. The ticking of the sunburst clock seemed deafening and when the doorbell rang, slashing into the silence, Zee almost jumped out of her skin. Frowning, she went into the hall. Earlier she had slipped the security chain across the door, and now she was grateful she had. It was far too early for Carol and Struan to have returned, and her heart began to pound as she turned the catch. Who would be foolish enough to be out on such a dreadful night? Switching on the porch light, she opened the door a crack.

'Hello.' Lorn was stood on the doorstep, looming tall in the lamplight. Snowflakes glistened in his hair and moustache, and the sheepskin jacket, over his suit, was flecked with damp patches of melting snow.

Her mouth dropped open. 'Wh-what are you doing here? I understood you were driving down to Birmingham,' she stammered, clinging on to the edge of the door with blood-drained knuckles.

He stamped his feet, rubbing his hands together, shivering in the cold. 'I decided to take a leaf out of your book and change my mind,' he said, the corner of his mouth lifting. 'You are going to let me in, aren't you? I'm in danger of freezing solid! I've been pacing up and down this path for ages, trying to pluck up the courage to ring the bell.' He blew on his hands, his breath cloudy-white on the night air. 'There are my tracks,' he told her, jerking back his head.

There was a well-worn trail in the snow.

'What do you want?' Zee asked warily.

'First, to come inside.' He flicked his fingers at the chain. 'Move it.'

Numbly she unhooked the chain and opened the door. Lorn stamped his feet a few times to clear the snow from his shoes, and strode into the hall. Zee took a backward step to allow him to pass her, but he didn't. Instead he firmly shut the door behind him and placed both hands flat on the wall on either side of her head, imprisoning her. In the bulky jacket he seemed larger than ever. Zee turned her head from side to side, but the gesture only made him lean closer. There was no escape.

'And secondly. . . .'

Bending his elbows, he lowered himself against her, squashing her slender body beneath him. His lips were ice-cold, but at their touch a wave of yearning swept over her. Gentle and coaxing, his mouth took heat from hers, and of their own volition Zee's lips parted. Snowflakes on his moustache melted, but went unnoticed as the body heat grew between them. With breathtaking thoroughness, he ransacked the velvet of her mouth until Zee began to tremble.

'No, Lorn. I don't want to make love, not . . .' she paused, 'not on a one-off basis.' She raised her hands to his chest, pushing him away.

With a sigh he forced himself upright. 'Come out to dinner with me, then we can try and. . . .' He arched a thick brow. 'Compromise? Isn't that the name of the game?'

'It's much too late to go out to dinner. In any case, I can't. I'm babysitting while Carol and Struan are at a dance. Look at me,' her gaze swept downwards over her amber velour dressing-gown. 'I'm ready for bed.'

'So I see,' he grinned, eyes touring her body beneath the clinging material. 'Go to bed, then. You can squeeze up and make room for me, though I doubt you'll get much in the way of beauty sleep.'

'Be serious,' she muttered, not quite knowing whether he meant it or not. The darkly seductive gleam in his eyes was unsettling her. Previously she had always been aware of him controlling the desire between them, refusing to allow it to develop into something more than he could handle, but this morning had revealed a different side to Lorn. . . .

Chewing anxiously at her lip, as she considered this new development, Zee led the way into the lounge.

'I've been serious for far too long,' said Lorn as he followed her. 'You told me to loosen up a little, and you were right. I've decided to follow your instructions.' Discarding his sheepskin jacket, he tugged at his tie, easing the knot.

'I didn't mean you should do a striptease,' she retorted, watching in dismay as he removed his suit jacket and unfastened the top button of his shirt.

He laughed softly. 'How far am I allowed to go?'

The erotic words sent quivers of desire rippling over her body, but she edged primly away when he sat down beside her on the settee.

'I don't know what you thought I was offering you in London, Lorn, but it wasn't casual sex. I realise now that my suggestion we live together was unwise and impetuous, but it wasn't flippant. I—I don't sleep around.'

'I'm well aware of that, my darling,' he murmured, lacing his fingers with hers. Zee looked down at their joined hands. Her skin seemed so soft and pale against his lean hard brownness.

'I never intended Mike and me to—well . . .' she half-shrugged suddenly embarrassed, 'to make love before we were married. At the time it seemed a great idea for him to join Tricia and me at the flat, but as usual I was jumping in with both feet. I never saw it as an open invitation for him to share my bed, but Mike thought otherwise. We had some awful arguments, but in the end I gave way.'

'And you regretted it?'

'He was always mauling me.' Zee shuddered at the memory. 'It was horrible! He didn't give a damn about *my* feelings, all he cared about was his own satisfaction.'

'Wham, bam, thank you, ma'am?' Lorn said drily, slipping his arm around her, wishing he could kiss the pain from her brow. If only he had met her before this bloody Mike. . . .

Zee swallowed hard. 'Yes. So I left as soon as I possibly could and decided it was a darn sight more sensible to be a career woman than be subjected to the selfish desires of some man.'

'And now you're going to New York,' said Lorn, trying not to care.

'N-no.'

'Not yet,' he remarked flatly. 'But you will. I had a drink with the personnel guy from the Americana group, and he told me he'd had an application from a young woman who sounded eminently suitable.'

'It wasn't me.'

'What do you mean?' he demanded, suddenly angry with her. God, he'd instructed Miles to tell her about the vacancy, what was she playing at now?

'I never applied.'

'Why the hell not?' His blue eyes glittered with impatience. 'It's perfect for you—interesting workload, excellent salary, good prospects and international travel. Burt Loren, the Chief Executive, is a dynamic fellow, a real go-getter. You'd enjoy working with him.'

'You sound as though you want to get rid of me, travelling around the world,' she accused miserably.

Lorn sighed. 'At least if you worked for them I'd be able to keep an eye on you. Several of their hotels are in the same locations as Devenay ones.'

'And why would you want to keep an eye on me?' she demanded.

'Because you're not safe to be left alone, you stupid bloody woman,' he growled. 'You need me around as a steadying influence. I'll help to keep your feet on the ground.'

'Like a pair of concrete boots?' she flared.

Lorn sank his head into his hands, running his fingers through the hair at his temples. 'Oh, God, no!' he groaned. 'I realise now I can't own you. I just want you on your own terms, Zee.' He frowned. 'Why didn't you apply? You haven't found some other job, have you? Something abroad?' There was a note of panic he couldn't disguise.

'No,' she assured him, placing her hand on his arm. The look of torment in his eyes was ripping into her heart. 'I haven't reached any decisions. I'm thinking once, twice and three times before I take the next step. The Americana job sounds rather lonely. I know on the surface it appears exciting,' she continued, as he turned to face her, 'but when you look beyond the glamour, it could add up to a series of lonely nights in strange hotels, with people you don't give a damn about.'

Lorn narrowed his eyes. 'But you have to accept these conditions if you're ambitious. You have to make sacrifices. It's not all beer and skittles.'

'Supposing I'm not prepared to live like that?' she asked, raising a brow.

His shoulders moved. 'Then you might as well forget the whole idea.'

Zee edged closer to him. 'Perhaps I will,' she said huskily.

Lorn held himself stiffly as her fingers moved to his shirt. Slowly she loosened one button, and then the next.

'You mean you don't intend to be a career woman?' he asked, frowning.

'Not one hundred per cent,' she said, when all the buttons were freed. She tugged his shirt from his trousers. 'I'd like to work for another year or two, and then—who knows?'

His arms slid around her, holding her so tightly she could feel the heavy thud of his heart.

'So you'll marry me?' he asked, realisation slowly dawning, lifting his mouth into a smile. Before Zee could reply there was the harsh jangle of the telephone in the hall.

'I must answer it before it disturbs the children,' she gasped, pushing herself from his arms and making for the door. Lorn followed, and as she lifted the receiver he pulled her close, fumbling to untie the sash of her robe. His tongue traced the pink lobe of her ear.

'Zee, it's me,' Carol announced worriedly. 'Look, the snow's very thick here and it's still falling. Struan thinks it would be wiser if we stayed the night at the hotel, rather than risk icy roads in the dark. Would that be okay with you?'

'Fine,' she murmured weakly. Lorn had slipped the robe from her shoulders and was now stroking the tilted curve of her breasts beneath the silken bodice of her nightgown. His mouth had deserted her ear, tracing a moistly eager path down her throat, eliminating lucid thought.

'We'll be home first thing in the morning,' Carol continued. 'Are you sure you're all right? You sound rather breathless.'

'I'm fine,' Zee repeated, giving a little gasp as Lorn pulled aside the silken bodice, exposing her full pointed breasts. Flicking deliciously with his tongue, he began arousing her with consummate skill, until her jutting nipples ached with desire. She dropped down the telephone.

'Tell me you'll marry me,' he said, raising his head from her.

'Yes, darling. Yes, yes!' she said, delirious with happiness.

With a murmur of satisfaction Lorn lifted her into his arms and carried her upstairs to the darkness of her bedroom. Her arms were entwined around his neck as he laid her on the bed, and she refused to abandon him.

'Let me get undressed, Zee,' he pleaded softly, and she felt the smile through his lips on her neck. Her hands joined his as he pulled off his clothes, then he slipped her nightgown over her head, and their naked bodies were together.

'*God*—Zee!' It was a sob, deep in his throat. 'I've wanted to be naked with you for so long, my darling, and now ...' he swore in anguish, 'now I can hardly wait!'

Rolling from her, he took several steadying breaths regaining control, then his mouth was on her breasts, her hips, her thighs, sensually kissing, licking, teasing. Lighting such fires of fierce desire that Zee hardly knew what she was going. Now instinct made her touch and pleasure him until he moaned aloud.

'I must have been crazy to let you go in London,' he muttered.

Like his mouth, his fingers were everywhere, caressing, touching, stroking, circling on her sensitive skin, until Zee arched her back, lost in a giant whirlpool of sensuality. She moulded her limbs to his in an open invitation to the scorching surge of his masculinity, aching to feel him. It had never been like this with Mike, she thought dimly. Never this need which was racking her body in the most tantalising way possible.

She cried out in the darkness. 'Please, Lorn. Please!'

With a tortured groan he invaded her, moving slowly, washing her with tide upon tide of desire as she clung to him, fingers feverishly raking his broad shoulders. When the climax came, it was like a beautiful wave breaking over her, dripping down her arms and legs, to the utmost extremities of her body. As it drained away she was left panting, stranded on a shore of contented lethargy. Lorn had given her a gift of sensual satisfaction she had never dreamed possible.

'Darling,' she whispered reverently, as he lay against her, his breath warm against her skin.

'I love you,' he said, pulling the blankets over them.

The aftermath was sweet. Zee snuggled happily against his shoulder.

'Let's get married as quickly as possible,' he said when he could think straight. 'I may have made you pregnant, and if I have I would rather we didn't wait too long.' He gave a self-deprecating grin. 'You know I'm not really in favour of babies being born before the socially accepted span of time, even if they are called love children.'

Zee ran a finger across his moustache. 'There's no need to worry. I am on the pill, *and* I'm taking it regularly.'

'Oh.' He was nonplussed.

'I'm not completely scatterbrained,' she pouted, pulling at the blond whiskers and making him wince. 'I realised early on that I could be vulnerable as far as you were concerned. It seemed wise to take precautions. I do think ahead sometimes.'

'Oh,' he said again, then he recovered. 'Please will you work with me on the remainder of the Devenay projects?'

'Isn't that called nepotism?' she teased.

Lorn caught at her fingers and kissed them, one by one.

'You can call it nepotism. I'll call in indulgence,' he smiled.

'Have you decided whether or not to give Edgar a firm answer, and take up a seat on the board?'

He kissed her brow. 'I've decided to accept nothing but the Chairmanship. I can't work under Edgar, there's no point pretending I can. If I accept merely a directorship I'll be champing at the bit all the time, wanting to do things *my* way. It's bound to result in a hell of a lot of aggro, so I'm going to aim straight for the top.'

'Is Mr Edgar prepared to stand down?' she asked in surprise.

The corner of Lorn's mouth twitched. 'Not yet, but I have a suspicion that over the next year or so he might just decide he's really happier playing golf than working in an office. It'll be a slow process, but I reckon he'll get used to the idea if I drop him a hint or two.'

'Then you'll pounce?'

'Mmm.' He buried his face in her hair. 'Do you think we could stop talking now?'

For a few glorious minutes he devoted himself to the task of kissing every inch of her warm womanly skin, then, as Zee was beginning to ache again, he raised his head abruptly.

'Oh dear! What will your sister and her husband think when they find me here in the morning?'

He looked so anxious that Zee laughed. Pushing her fingers into the thick blond hair at the nape of his neck, she pulled him back to her. 'I really have no idea, sir,' she grinned, and waited to receive her punishment.

A very special gift for Mother's Day

You love Mills & Boon romances. Your mother will love this attractive Mother's Day gift pack. First time in paperback, four superb romances by leading authors. A very special gift for Mother's Day.

United Kingdom £4.40   On sale from 24th Feb 1984

A Grand Illusion
Maura McGiveny

Sensual Encounter
Carole Mortimer

Desire in the Desert
Mary Lyons

Aquamarine
Madeleine Ker

Look for this gift pack where you buy
Mills & Boon romances.

FREE
An exciting
Mills & Boon
Romance

Spare a few moments to answer the questions
overleaf and we will send you an exciting
Mills & Boon Romance as our
special thank you.

A NEW YEAR AND
A NEW LOOK!

We all think our new look covers are even
more attractive and romantic.

But that's not good enough!
We want to know what you think.

Tell us – honestly – and we will send you
an exciting **Mills & Boon Romance**.

Just tick the answers to the three simple
questions overleaf. And don't forget to fill
in your name and address – so that we
know where to send your
free Mills & Boon book.

**Fill in and post this page
today – no stamp needed** **see over**

JUST TICK THE ANSWERS FOR YOUR FREE BOOK:

1 Have you ever read a Mills & Boon Romance before?

◻ Yes ◻ No

a If you have, do you like the new cover design?

◻ Yes ◻ No ◻ No Difference

b If you haven't, were you attracted to this book by the cover design?

◻ Yes ◻ No ◻ Made no impression

2 What do you think is the most important element in the cover design? (Tick one only)

◻ a) The colour ◻ b) The author's name
◻ c) The series' name ◻ d) The illustration
◻ e) The title ◻ f) The publisher's name

3 What made you buy this book? (Tick one only)

◻ a) The author ◻ b) The description of the story
◻ c) The illustration ◻ d) The publisher's name
◻ e) The series' name

Is there anything you particularly like or dislike about this cover? _____

_____

Fill in your name and address, put this page in an envelope (you can fold it if you need to) and post today to:
Mills & Boon Reader Survey, FREEPOST, P.O. Box 236, Croydon CR9 9EL, Surrey.

NO STAMP NEEDED

Name _____

Address _____

_____

_____ Postcode _____